W9-ARH-633

The Piano Tuner

Winner of
The Flannery O'Connor Award
For Short Fiction

The Piano Tuner

Stories by
Peter Meinke

The University
of Georgia Press
Athens and London

MIDDLEBURY COLLEGE LIBRARY

PS
3563
.E348
P5
1986

© 1986 by Peter Meinke
Published by the University of Georgia Press
Athens, Georgia 30602
All rights reserved

Designed by Betty P. McDaniel
Set in 10 on 13 Trump Mediaeval with Gill Sans display

The paper in this book meets the guidelines for
permanence and durability of the Committee on
Production Guidelines for Book Longevity of the
Council on Library Resources.

Printed in the United States of America

90 89 88 87 86   5 4 3 2 1

Library of Congress Cataloging in Publication Data

Meinke, Peter.
  The piano tuner.

  I. Title.
PS3563.E348P5   1986   813'.54   85-28864
ISBN 0-8203-0844-7 (alk. paper)

For Jeanne

Acknowledgments

The author and the publisher gratefully acknowledge the magazines and anthologies in which some of the stories in this volume first appeared.

"The Piano Tuner" and "The Twisted River" were published in the *Atlantic Monthly,* and "The Piano Tuner" was subsequently selected for inclusion in *The Best American Short Stories 1985* (Houghton Mifflin).

"Losers Pay" first appeared in the *Carleton Miscellany.*

"Even Crazy Old Barmaids Need Love" was originally published in *Gallery.*

"A Decent Life" first appeared in the *Virginia Quarterly Review.*

"Alice's Brother," "The Ponoes," "Conversation with a Pole," and "The Bracelet" were published in *Yankee,* and "The Ponoes" was selected for inclusion in *Prize Stories 1983: The O'Henry Awards* (Doubleday & Company).

"Ruby Lemons" first appeared in *From Mt. San Angelo: Stories, Poems, and Essays* (Associated University Presses).

Contents

I Home Thoughts
The Piano Tuner   3
Alice's Brother   15
Ruby Lemons   23
The Ponoes   34
Conversation with a Pole   46
Losers Pay   58
Even Crazy Old Barmaids Need Love   71

II From Abroad
A Decent Life   85
The Twisted River   97
Sealink   108
The Starlings of Leicester Square   117
Winter Term   122
The Water-Tree   134
The Bracelet   144

I
Home Thoughts

The Piano Tuner

The piano tuner was a huge man, crowding the doorway. I hadn't known he was coming, but I got up from my desk to let him in; my wife was still out shopping. His head was small for his body, and his belt was almost hidden by the belly folding over it. I suppose I came up to about his shoulders, and the reek of his sweat was stunning. His stained T-shirt announced THE PIANO EXCHANGE.

"Where's the piano?" he said.

"In there." I pointed toward the music room. "But there's nothing much wrong with it."

"Yeah, we'll see." His voice resonated like the bass in a barbershop quartet.

I led him through the living room to the small music room. In one corner the mahogany of my wife's Russian-made harp glowed in the late-afternoon sunlight. By the casement windows on the right stood my old piano, painted black. "It's an 1899 Kimball," I told him. I was proud of this handsome antique, with its scrolled legs and matching bench.

"No, it's not that old," the piano tuner said sourly, "but it looks like a Kimball all right."

"It *says* Kimball." I pointed to the gold lettering.

He bent over the keys, shaking his little head. "That means shit. This'll take some time; I'll go get my tools." He

straightened up with a sudden intake of breath, as if someone had kicked him in a kidney. "Jesus," he said.

I wanted to go back to my desk to continue my work. Fredericks would be furious if my review was late again, but this
one was proving particularly troublesome. The problem was,
I knew all the authors; there was no one I could attack with
relative impunity. Van Buren was clearly the weakest, but he
had said such good things about *my* last book, I had to re-
ciprocate somewhat. Prokol was a friend of Fredericks's. I
had just about decided to stick it to Foreman, who was pretty
good but without influence, when the piano tuner rang.

I wished my wife wouldn't make these appointments
without telling me. Besides, it was my piano and it sounded
all right to me. I had been practicing Durand's "Valse," a not-
too-difficult but flashy piece with lots of runs on the right
hand and oompah on the left, and I hadn't noticed anything.
Maybe the B-flat stuck a little now and then. I practiced hard
when my wife was out, though I pretended never to practice
at all. She was a pretty good harpist, but had to work hard
at it.

I wouldn't feel right going back to my study with this
massive lout of a piano tuner lumbering through the house.
Who was he to say my piano was not that old? We had a
lot of expensive—irreplaceable, really—souvenirs scattered
around; he might just slip our Wedgwood ashtray into his
pocket, or a wooden plate from Poland into the khakis
bunched below his gargantuan stomach. Where was he, anyway? I looked out the front door. He was standing in our
driveway, next to a dilapidated VW van, talking to a thin black
man about half his size. The van's windows were painted
crudely, in childlike strokes, with a continuous forest scene;
on the back were what appeared to be the turrets of a castle.
Whenever a car wandered down our narrow, curving street,
the black man would lean back and deliver a sharp karate-
style kick toward the car, which would swerve to the other

side and then move on. The piano tuner paid no attention to this but kept talking intently, crouched over, fingers jabbing the air. When he saw me watching, he called out, "Help me with these, will you?" I noticed two large metal toolboxes at his feet.

The thought occurred to me that there were just two boxes and he had two hands, but his tone was so peremptory that I walked down the driveway to comply. Up close, the black man was startling to look at: the skin on his face, arms, and hands had large, irregular patches of pink. I was consciously not staring at him, but he said, "What you lookin' at, man?" Of course, I didn't reply, and turned to the piano tuner instead.

"If I was a little more diseased," the black man said, stepping between us, "I be white like you." He leaned away, aiming his foot at me, but as I jumped backward he reversed and bent steeply toward me, snapping his foot behind him into the side of the van, leaving a good-sized dent.

The piano tuner had already started toward the house, carrying one of the toolboxes as lightly as if it were empty, and he didn't turn around. I hefted the other one and lurched after him. "Watch out for the flowers!" I shouted, not knowing whether to look in front or in back of me. His great square-toed boot had just crushed one of our azalea cuttings alongside the driveway. I had told my wife it was asking for trouble, planting them so close to where people walk, but she was an incurable optimist, believing somehow that everyone would be careful and sensible, would keep within the proper boundaries. Twice a year she pruned our azaleas, potting the cuttings for two months in just the proper mixture of vermiculite and peat moss before transferring them to various parts of our property in her ongoing beautification program. She was the neighborhood's answer to Lady Bird Johnson.

The piano tuner paused on the doorstep, waiting for me to

open the door for him. "My wife loves azaleas," I said, "so please be careful of them."

"I don't like flowers, myself," he said. "They bother my asthma." I had already noticed his heavy breathing. With a sinking heart I opened the door and led him in, trying to get him to follow my example of not stepping on our delicate Persian rugs, mementos of our year in Iran. But he blindly and heavily—greasily, muddily—tramped straight across them into the music room. With surprising dexterity and speed for such a heavy man he had the top and front panels of the piano off in a minute. The exposed keys huddled together like ranks of suddenly naked soldiers. He set up the tuning hammer and began hitting single notes over and over.

"I think it's all right," I said.

"It's flat," he replied, without looking at me. "I'll have to bring it up almost a whole tone. That'll cost you fifty dollars."

"Sometimes the B-flat sticks," I said, trying to show some knowledgeability about the subject. I could read music, but I was tone-deaf; his jarring notes meant nothing to me.

"Yeah, you need some new hammers. Some turkey tried to fix them with Scotch tape. That'll cost extra." I could see the dried-out tape peeling off the pegs like old gauze bandages. The piano tuner did not sit down but stood humped over the keyboard, left hand prodding the notes, right hand working the tuning hammer. His fingers were so large it was hard to believe he could press down a single key at a time.

I went back to my study but was unable to work in that comfortable, windowless room; the repetitive striking of notes was too irritating. At the same time I felt I needed the door open so I could keep an eye on the piano tuner, whom I instinctively mistrusted. After sitting immobile at my desk for what seemed hours, I got up and made myself a drink. What was keeping my wife? Evening was coming on. Looking out the living-room window, I saw the black man still in the driveway. Now he had headphones on, and an expensive-looking portable stereo sat against the pole supporting the basketball backboard our son had loved so much. The man was dancing to the silent music, making Oriental motions with his chin, neck, and hands, not unlike his earlier karate movements.

I walked over to the music room. "That man is still out there," I announced somewhat superfluously, since he could be clearly seen through the casement windows.

"It's a free country," said the piano tuner, looking up. Rivulets of sweat ran down his face, and his thin hair gleamed on the bullet-shaped head. Dark wet spots patched his T-shirt, and his chin was going black with stubble, rougher and thicker than when he arrived. He was staring at my drink.

"Do you want a glass of water, or a beer?" I asked.

"No," he said, "maybe a little whiskey. Beer hurts my stomach. You got some Jim Beam or something?"

"I've got a little bourbon, I forget what it is."

"Sure, a little bourbon, it's good for the digestion. My digestion is terrible."

"Have you eaten?" I said. My conversation seemed to pop out of me against my will.

He pulled on the tuner with a grunt. "No, when could I eat? I'll eat later, I'm used to it. I meant to say, if a string breaks, you got to pay for that, too."

When I brought him his drink, he sat down with a sigh, hiking his pants up tight around his crotch. I asked him how long the tuning would take; if it was going to take too long, maybe he should come back another day.

"No," he said, "you got to work nights, overtime, if you're a piano tuner. And even then, you can't afford to buy a woman." He banged the piano so hard that some whiskey splashed out of his glass.

I spoke smiling into the silence, trying to be man to man. "I didn't know people still had to buy women nowadays."

He looked at me as if I had thrown up on his boots. "Are

7

you kiddin'? Do you live under a rock, or what? Y'ever been downtown, see those babes on the street corners? What d'you think they are, goddamn city engineers?" He finished his bourbon in a gulp. "These felts are all eaten by roaches," he continued, peering into the piano. "That's going to cost ya."

I looked over his shoulder: the felt pads were indeed ragged and in places completely gone.

"And if you don't buy a woman," he went on, "you get in terrible trouble. I had a best friend once, and I was getting it on with his old lady; they had four kids. When he found out about it he just up and left, after twenty years! Took the car, too. God knows where he went." The piano tuner's sweat was splashing on the keys as he tightened the strings; his lower lip stuck out as though he might burst into tears, or maybe he was just pouting at the world's injustices, or straining with the effort of his work.

"Look," I said, "don't feel bad. If you could ruin a marriage like that, it probably wasn't worth saving anyway. It would've collapsed sooner or later. Don't blame yourself."

"Yeah," he said. "We're all going to die sooner or later, so I might as well strangle you now."

There was another silence while he stared at me. I was trying to smile.

"Am I right?" he said.

I couldn't believe my wife wasn't home yet. It was past supper time. This had happened before, but she had always left something in the oven for me. It wasn't like her to be so careless. I kept looking around, half expecting her to materialize through the walls.

The piano tuner sat down again and groped a cigarette out of a wrinkled pack. I dashed out to the kitchen for one of our old glass ashtrays and brought it to him. "My wife and I are trying to give up smoking," I explained.

"People who smoke have more lead in their pencil," he

said with conviction. "What do you think of just four smokes a day?"

"I heard you could smoke up to six a day without bad effects, but I could never hold myself down to that few." The smoke from his cigarette was making me dizzy; some of his ashes fell on the keys.

"I have four a day," he said. "I can't afford to get sick, but you gotta have something to enjoy."

"Yes, everyone does."

"The rich don't get sick. They get all the women they want, and good food, too. The poor get exercise and diet."

"It's a tough life," I said, trying to back out.

"Could be worse." He hit a few chords on the piano. "I pass blood every day, but they won't give me one of those scans, I don't know why. I did five push-ups three days in a row and I haven't recovered. I told the doc I'm a right-handed piano tuner, I can't afford to get arthritis in my right hand."

"How's the piano sounding?" I asked, trying to switch the conversation to more professional ground.

He ran a series of scales, starting from the bass and winding up high in the treble. "Some uprights are lemons, but this old Kimball is worth keeping up. I know a guy that refinished one and sold it for twenty-nine hundred dollars. The dampers are stuck, though," he said, working the pedals. "That has to be extra, too."

By now it was dark out. I brought him another bourbon. "How long is this going to take?" I asked.

"A long time," he wheezed, pulling on the tuner. "This is really flat. I have to bring it up a long way. It could take all night, but after nine o'clock I get double time."

This was a depressing prospect in several ways, so I said, "I don't know if I can afford it."

"Listen, it's worth it. This is a good instrument here. Almost as good as that harp." The harp looked outrageously expensive in the soft light.

"Well, we got that in Russia," I said. "It wasn't too expensive over there."

"Over here it's plenty expensive; this is real money," he said, waving his hand around. "You know, that harp's got over two thousand moving parts?" He peered backward toward the harp. "And that's gut string, the real thing. A lot of dead animals in this room, I'll tell you. Look"—he lifted his sloping shoulders with a groan—"I could use another bourbon." He had swallowed it like water, but I was ready for another one myself, so I went obediently to the kitchen.

After I got him the drink—a small one this time; I didn't want a drunken piano tuner on my hands—I went back to my study and sat down. I was worried about my wife. She really was very dependable. I had been taking her too much for granted, getting irritated by her high nasal voice, which, after all, was hardly her fault. She was still very attractive. When she came home, I would tell her that. She had probably gone to a matinee with Iris and they had stayed to discuss the movie over a bite to eat. I hated talking about movies. I never knew what to say. But why hadn't she called me? On impulse I got up and went to the phone. I had avoided it before because the phone was on the wall near the music room and it was somehow embarrassing to be looking for my wife in front of the piano tuner. He was working on the higher register now. Iris's line was busy. He hadn't paused while I was dialing, but when I hung up he stopped and the quiet was a great relief from the insanely repetitious notes.

"I've got a Reserve meeting tomorrow," I told him. "I have to find out what time I should leave." This was true enough, though my reluctance to speak about my wife in front of him puzzled me.

"You in the Army?" he asked.

"Yes," I said, 'I'm a captain in the Reserve. It brings in some nice extra income." At once I regretted saying that; he seemed to make me babble like an idiot.

"Were you in the war?" he asked.

"Yes, but I was stationed in Washington, reading documents."

"I was in the Navy in the sixties, during Vietnam." The piano tuner sighed. "Didn't do much, but you know what I liked?" His square-tipped left fingers kept striking notes while his right hand pulled the tuning key to tighten the strings. His little head bent close to the keys. "I liked laying in bed listening to the engine and feeling it shake the bunk, like a big cat purring or something. Sometimes I'd wake up and there'd be this little bird outside my porthole movin' right along with the ship without wavin' its wings or anything, just like it was painted there, its little black feet tucked under its belly like miniature bombs. That was a helluva way to sleep." He stood up, gasping, suddenly towering over me. "Now I got me a bad back and nobody gives a shit. Look, you got a vacuum? I need to clean the inside of this thing."

"Sure, in the bedroom upstairs. I'll get it for you."

"No need." With the swiftness that kept catching me off guard, he stepped by me onto the stair landing. "I got to stretch these legs." As soon as he disappeared I called Iris again; this time the phone rang, but there was no answer.

It was totally dark by now. I peered out the window. The van squatted like an armored car in the driveway, the streetlamp throwing the trees' shadows across it like camouflage; no one was near it. The piano tuner was using the bathroom upstairs, so I made myself a stiff drink and sat down in my study to wait him out. If only my wife were here! It came to me that she was the one who threw people out of the house—that was *her* job. She slammed the door in salesmen's faces, hung up on telephone solicitors. While I had a reputation as a stinging, even withering, critic, I was not programmed for face-to-face confrontations. I had even been known to lie on the kitchen floor while the Seventh Day

Adventists prowled our neighborhood with their books, leaflets, and sermons; the alternative, for me, was suffering through a dreary, hour-long lecture-debate. My wife, on the other hand, would just give them the raspberry and send them on their way.

Now the vacuum cleaner was going, and I breathed a relieved sigh. It must be almost over. A man's home *is* his castle, after all. I settled down at my typewriter and tried to concentrate on the review. After a while I was aware that the piano tuner was padding to the kitchen and back again, but I was determined to ignore him. Time passed, though I got little done. I found myself thinking about when I first met my wife. She stood at the top of a staircase in a summer dress, her eyes bright with energy and goodwill, her long legs tan and slim. No one expected more from the world than she, and right then and there I resolved that I would get it for her. Now, looking around, I realized I didn't even have a picture of her on my desk, just one of our son shooting baskets in the driveway. I remembered how the endless bouncing of that ball had driven me crazy.

Suddenly the piano burst into song: the piano tuner was playing, of all things, "The Battle Hymn of the Republic." "Mine eyes have seen the glory of the coming of the Lord . . ." His low voice accompanied the piano. I stuck my checkbook into my back pocket and walked to the music room. The piano was still apart and the bottle of bourbon sat beside the vacuum cleaner; the tools were spread across the floor—I couldn't believe the mess.

"I thought you were finished!" I shouted. I almost felt like crying.

"God, I love this song," he said, his deep voice slurred. He was playing it slowly, ponderously. "Listen, what do you think of it?"

"It's all right," I said, dragged in again, trying to control myself, thinking of the best way to get rid of him. "I've always liked the sound of the words, like *vintage* . . ."

"No! No! I mean it makes me feel like flying the flag, you know what I mean? Gettin' out there, marchin' down the streets." He struck the chords again.

"Well." I tried to smile, humoring him. "I've never been what you call patriotic, 'My country right or wrong' . . ."

The piano tuner swiveled toward me and glared.

"Look," I said, "you're through. You must be tired. I know I am. Let me pay you and you can go home."

"I haven't done the felts yet; that's a big job. That'll cost quite a bit. I just vacuumed the old felts out of here."

"Look," I repeated, "that's enough. You've been here long enough today. Call us tomorrow and we'll make an appointment for you to finish."

He picked up the bottle and sloshed some whiskey into his glass. He took a large sip and began to cough. His face turned purplish red. "Don't bother me," he said between coughs. "I'll just put the felts in. We got a contract."

"What contract? There isn't any contract, for God's sake!" I put my hand on his shoulder, where his crumpled cigarettes were rolled up in his T-shirt sleeve, the way tough high school kids had carried them in the fifties.

He sprang up and staggered through the debris on the floor, miraculously missing the bourbon bottle. He held me two inches above the elbow. "You just work at your desk till I finish," he said, propelling me across the living room. The only way for me to resist would have been to twist around and hit him or to sag to the floor. Naturally, I did neither.

"You'll get in trouble, you know," I said, feeling cowardly and humiliated. But he was a hundred pounds heavier than I was; what was I supposed to do? He gave me one last shove, a flick of his thick and hairy wrist, and I stumbled into my office. The door banged shut behind me and the key, always in the keyhole, turned in the lock. He had locked me in my own office! For the first time in several hours I was no longer nervous or afraid—just furious. I banged on the door, I shook it, I kicked it. Suddenly it swung open. The thought occurred to me that he was joking—this was the idiot's sense of humor, but I was not amused.

He was standing right there, of course, and I said, "*Get out of my house,*" with all the force I could muster. Like a frog snatching a fluttering moth, his right hand shot out and caught my left. He bent my little finger in on itself and the joints popped as I sank down on my knees. I felt a searing pain in my neck and dug my fingers under the piano wire he had looped over my head. He jerked me to my feet, four of my fingers still under the wire.

"Listen, the next time you bother me I'll pop your eyes out," he whispered. He shoved me back into the study and locked the door.

I lay on the floor a long time. For a while the piano tuner played as if bashing the piano with his fists. Keys were breaking, wood splintering, in some sort of devil's symphony. Radio music, turned up, competed with the piano. Absurdly I thought: What will the neighbors think? Where are my neighbors? And I remembered that I didn't even know their names. After some time I became aware of my own sobbing, and something else, frail and familiar. I rolled over and put my ear to the door. Under the din I could hear my wife's voice. "Oh," she was saying. When had she come in? "Oh, my God," she cried. "Oh! Oh!"

Alice's Brother

Alice's brother Dan had been a smoker all his life and had just had a laryngectomy to treat the cancer in his throat. They took out his voice box, but he refused to let them insert an artificial one.

"You talk to him," said Cynthia, Dan's second wife. "He won't listen to me. He just sits there and stares out the window. I told him he might as well be dead."

"Don't say things like that to him," said Alice. "But how can I talk to him? He can't say anything back." Alice lived in Boston and Cynthia had called from their country house in Vermont, where Dan was recuperating from his operation.

"It doesn't matter, he doesn't have to say anything. You know how he listens to you." Cynthia always said this in a resentful way, as if adding an unspoken *for some reason*. "Look, talk to him, will you? I know those boxes sound terrible, like an old World War I radio, but I can't live with this silence. It's a creep-house around here."

It occurred to Alice that *she* could live with silence, especially Dan's silence. What was the problem? They had been close since they were children, Dan two years younger than she. They didn't have to gab a lot to understand one another.

"All right, Cynthia, put him on. I don't know what I'll say."

"Thanks, Alice. Just give him a pitch. Tell him for Christ's sake *everybody's* getting voice boxes these days."

Images of her brother with his slim blond good looks tumbled through Alice's mind while Cynthia went to get him, though in truth he was no longer either slim or blond. Despite his smoking and drinking, Dan had had a wonderful singing voice, a fine Irish tenor; no wonder he didn't want a tinny voice box. On the other hand, you couldn't just go through life like a deaf-mute, especially if, like Dan, you always thought of funny things to say. Maybe he could write them out. What was she going to tell him?

"Alice," Cynthia said, "here's Dan. Please put some sense into his stubborn head."

She could hear the phone changing hands, shuffling of feet, the scraping of a chair. "Dan. How are you?" she said, remembering right away that he couldn't answer. Stupid! "I'm so sorry you're having trouble. I wish I were there to help you." There was a sound like a mouse scratching. Was he trying to say something? She had heard that people with voice boxes could still whistle, maybe they could make other sounds as well.

"Dan, is there anything you'd like me to do? God, I keep forgetting! Look, we can't do it this way, I just can't make a speech at you. You'll do what you want to, anyway, just like you always have. Let's do this, I have an idea," she said. "I'll ask you questions, and you tap once for Yes and twice for No. Is that all right? I'm supposed to talk to you about this voice box."

After a brief pause Alice said, "Do you have a pencil or something?"

Tap. Yes!

"Oh, Dan, isn't this a good idea!"

Tap-tap. No.

"No?" she cried. "Why not? Oh, that won't work!" She shook the phone in exasperation. "You don't want to talk?"

Tap-tap. No.

She realized she would have trouble with negative questions, so she asked again. "Do you want to talk?"

Tap-tap.

"But Dan," Alice said, "you can't do this!" In the mirror by the phone she could see her eyes tearing up. Suddenly it seemed that the most important thing in the world was to somehow communicate with her brother. They had always loved one another, stayed in touch through all kinds of separations. He couldn't pull away now, just because of a stupid voice box!

"Dan, is Cynthia there? I don't want to talk to her or anything, I just want to know if she's there."

Tap-tap. No.

"Good. Are you sitting down?"

Tap. Yes.

"Good. I am, too." Alice paused, wrapping the telephone cord around her wrist the way the children did. "I want you to tell me everything. I think I know, anyway, but I want to hear it from you. With your own pencil." She smiled into the mirror; people always said she and Dan had twin smiles. "That's a joke." She paused again.

Tap.

"That's better. We can still joke together, can't we?"

Tap.

"Are you in pain? The truth."

Tap. Tap-tap.

"Yes and no? Sometimes?"

Tap.

"I don't think Cynthia helps you enough. She's never had children, she doesn't have that motherly instinct. Anyway, she's a child herself." Alice frowned at her gray hair in the mirror. "I can see that she's sexy and all that, but I think you know by now you made a big mistake. Eleanor was so nice, in her quiet sort of way."

There was no reply to this, so Alice asked, "Don't you agree?"

Tap.

"Listen, I'll tell you a joke. An old man dies and goes to heaven and Jesus is at the gate, giving St. Peter a break, I suppose. 'You look familiar,' says Jesus, 'were you a carpenter, by any chance?' 'Why, yes I was,' says the old man. 'Did you have a beloved son who went away and left you?' 'Alas, so I did,' the old man says. Jesus is getting very excited and says, 'And tell me, in the end, did that son have holes in his hands and feet?' 'Why, yes, he did. This is extraordinary!' 'Father!' cries Jesus, and the old man says, 'Pinocchio?' Do you think that's funny?"

Tap-tap.

"Well, I know you like your jokes spicier, but I can't tell those. It must be a cultural thing, don't you think? Wherever you go there are all these men telling wonderful jokes and the women just stand around and smile. You're so lucky. I think it's because men have been pampered, we're so busy taking care of you all our lives that we never develop a sense of humor. Do you think that's right?"

Tap.

Alice laughed. "Now I think *you're* joking! You never agree to statements like that. But maybe things are changing. The young women today are funnier, they don't care what they say. Still, Cynthia has no sense of humor at all."

Tap.

"You mean Yes she does, or Yes she has no sense of humor? Wait a minute. Does Cynthia have any sense of humor at all?"

Tap-tap.

"You poor baby, that's what I thought. And you the funniest person in the entire world! Are you in pain now? Right now?"

Tap. Yes. *Tap.* Yes.

"Oh, Dan! Very much pain?"

Tap.

"Is it this way most of the time?"

Tap.

"Why doesn't Cynthia do anything about it? There must be pills. No wonder you don't want a voice box, I don't blame you! You had such a beautiful voice, what is she thinking of?" Alice heard a chair scraping and asked, "Are you still there?"

Tap-tap.

She almost burst out sobbing: he *was* telling jokes! "Remember, Dan, when you sang at my wedding, it was so lovely everyone cried? I'll tell you a secret. You were so much handsomer than Charles I almost didn't go through with it."

Tap-tap.

"Of course you'd say no. I'm the only one who really appreciates you, including yourself. I knew there was a wild streak in you that Eleanor couldn't stand, but I liked that! I have one myself, though no one would ever know. If people knew what I really thought they'd be shocked to death, even the children. Diana keeps trying to sign me up for a workshop in Love, or Creativity, or Grace, or something wacko like that—she calls it 'attaining life-style excellence.' Where do the children learn to talk like that?" Alice stood up and began pacing around the hallway, holding the cord over her shoulder. "Dan, do you think we have souls?"

Tap-tap.

"See, I knew it, we agree on everything. No souls, no voice boxes," she said. "Oh, I'm sorry for saying that! I feel drunk or something. You know what I think? I think everything we don't do—take a trip to Greece, for example, eat a piece of chocolate cake, have an affair with a Turk—is always just that: something we didn't do. And then it's all over. What do you think? I mean, do you understand what I'm saying?"

Tap.

"I knew you would. I could never talk to Charles like this. 'I don't know, dear,' he'd always say, 'that depends.' And I'd say, 'Charles, don't you have a single goddamn opinion of your own? We either have souls or we don't have souls, one or the other!' And he'd say, 'Well, that depends on what you mean by soul . . .' He could go on forever like that, I would have been glad to shoot him!" Alice sat down again and leaned toward the mirror. "Still, I miss him, anyway. He wasn't a mean person, and you two got along so well. But then men always do, it must be some sort of trick. You have a drink, light each other's cigarettes, talk about some illiterate ballplayer, and immediately you're bosom buddies till the end of time. I don't think it's fair, life should be harder than that."

Tap.

"Dan, are you kidding with me? I want you to be serious. You know, I think I married Charles because he had such wonderful teeth, he was so good to kiss before we got married. I hate men with little crooked teeth. I never understood why people like that smile so much! Probably it's just nervousness. But the third night after we were married we were sitting in bed and I looked over at Charles and there he was flat-flossing his teeth right in front of me! The whole bed was shaking as if he were trying to dislodge boulders. I don't think I ever recovered from that. *You* would never have done such a thing, but then everyone in our family has good teeth without even trying. The only time I ever used flat floss— trying to be nice to Charles—I flipped my bridge out and it cost us four hundred dollars. That was that." Alice clenched her teeth and stretched wide her lips. "Does Cynthia use flat floss?"

Tap.

"I thought so. But she *is* a good-looking girl, there's no doubt about it. It's funny, though, I'm not the least bit jealous of her—she's simply too young. When you married Eleanor I was so jealous! I pretended to like her—I really *did* like her, in a way—but mainly I was jealous, isn't that silly? What did she know about what you liked and what you were like? And she was too shy to find out. If I had married you, you would never have divorced *me!*" Alice fumbled for her lipstick and began applying it carefully, squinting into the mirror. "Don't listen to me, I'm just babbling along. It's because I'm so worried about you." A random reflection made her lips look bright red, and she leaned back.

Tap.

"Dan, I had that dream again, you know the one where I'm in a long corridor and all the doors are exactly the same? But I know which one is mine, and my heart is beating so fast when I reach it I just can't stand it; and then I reach out and open it and it's completely empty, terrifyingly empty, and I scream and wake up. Do you ever have dreams like that?"

Tap-tap.

"But do you dream at all? Maybe men don't really dream like women, your psyches aren't developed enough, you basically stay little boys."

Tap.

"Yes, what? Yes, you stay little boys?"

Tap-tap.

"No? You mean, you do have dreams."

Tap.

"Are they good dreams?"

Tap-tap.

"Oh, Dan, I'm so sorry. Of course you have dreams, and of course they're terrible! I wish I could dream them for you, I wouldn't be afraid, I'm used to them, poor baby. I could dream of falling, down and down, into the darkest pits; I would do that for you. Flames and monsters. Giants. Dan, do you remember that day, God, it must be seven lifetimes ago, when Father came home and caught you smoking his cigars? You stood there, so pale and brave, and Father kept slapping you and slapping you until I jumped on his back and pulled his hair. No one was more surprised than me, except maybe Father! But I wasn't afraid. Oh, I don't know what to do. I'd do anything to help you, and here I am in Boston and you up there with Cynthia."

Alice stood up, walked to the narrow alcoved window, and sat down on the ledge. It was beginning to rain, and passersby hunched their shoulders and pulled their coats tight around their necks. She stared at her streaked reflection in the window, through which, it seemed to her, the dark apartments across the street were frowning.

"Dan, do you love me?"

Tap-tap.

"No, Dan!" she cried. "Don't do that! Tell me the truth. Do you love me more than any woman in the whole world?"

Tap.

Tap.

Tap. Tap. Tap. Alice put the receiver on her lap and opened the window, the slanting rain spotting her dress, tapping in gusts across the slippery ledge and over the pane.

Ruby
Lemons

"Ruby lemons," Jack gushed all at once, turning from his typewriter. "High ruby lemons." He smiled his crazy smile at Mr. Mason, shaking his head up and down. The monkey leaped from his lap to the top of the china closet without seeming to touch anything else. Three plates with pictures of churches on them were balanced on top of the closet and, leaning precariously against the wall, rolled back and forth as the monkey paced in front of them.

"Pesky, get down here!" Aunt Dodo cried. "He means high bilirubins. Jack has *always* had a high bilirubin count and they don't know what to do about it." They all turned to Jack; he looked down and shuffled his feet.

"He never gets it right," continued Aunt Dodo, while Aunt Lottie and Aunt Gussie smiled at Jack and he smiled hugely back. "But it always comes out like real words. He's a poet, is what he is." Jack all but nodded his head off his thin shoulders. "Poetry," he said.

"You know what Jack calls Miss Pennyfeather? Mrs. Ferry Weather!" said Aunt Gussie. The three gray-haired sisters laughed and Jack joined them with an explosive snort. "Ferry Weather!" he said, and turned back to his typing. Mr. Mason tried to smile, too. The monkey swung back down and settled in Jack's lap again, leaving the cups in the china closet swaying in unison on their hooks, like a line of chorus girls in hoopskirts. Two of the sisters *had* been chorus girls, if only briefly, and Aunt Lottie had been a lead singer in church groups and little theaters; they all were musical, even in their sixties and seventies. They liked nothing more than to gather around the small black spinet and sing the old songs again, with Aunt Lottie playing and Jack providing a surprisingly good, if erratic, male tenor. Jack suffered from cerebral palsy, but for some unknown reason music seemed to clear the blocked roadways of his brain and he could follow along with them, though he had a tendency to go on after the others had stopped, repeating, soulfully, "alive alive-o" at the end of "Cockles and Mussels" four or five times before realizing the music was over.

They lived in a tall gray skinny house in St. Paul, somewhat isolated because of vacant lots on either side and a practice field in the back that belonged to nearby Hamline University. In the summer several huge lilac bushes gave it a festive air, but in the long winter the wind banged the house so hard that its curtains blew as if the ancient windows were open. There were three small bedrooms upstairs, one for each sister; the downstairs was a classic example of shotgun architecture: from the front, four rooms lined up in a row— the living room (with the piano), dining room, kitchen, and, in the back, Jack's bedroom. He liked to sit at his window and watch the college girls run back and forth, flailing their field hockey sticks at the bounding ball. "Hole!" he would shout when one of the girls scored, as elated as she was.

Jack was twenty-seven and his interest in girls was as much a topic of conversation in the house as the high number of bilirubins in his blood. In fact, Uncle Frank used to say, when he caught Jack watching the girls, "Bilirubins a little randy today, eh, Jack boy?" The sisters were more sedate and circumspect, though they tried to interest some of the girls in coming to play checkers with Jack, because he enjoyed their company so much, and the sisters thought it was healthy, someone close to his own age. But one of the girls had got frightened, over nothing at all, and this had brought Miss Pennyfeather and the shadowy disturbance of the State into their lives.

Aunt Gussie, at sixty-four the smallest and youngest of the sisters, worked as a part-time librarian at Hamline, and the last girl she had brought home, a petite brunette sophomore named Thelma Freese, had been nervous from the start. Gussie had explained about the cerebral palsy and how Jack loved to play checkers and needed the company of young people, but his appearance had clearly startled her and, to be honest, Jack had been in one of his more manic moods. He had been one of those children who couldn't swallow, the muscles of his tongue and throat working backwards to propel the food out instead of in, and he still looked starved: when he was animated, his thin, twisted body jerked about like an emaciated puppet.

Most of the girls had been big tough farm girls from Minnesota who took his looks in stride and who could squeeze back when Jack surprised them with his powerful left-handed shake (although he could type with his right hand, he had difficulty raising it). As Aunt Lottie would say, these girls didn't know diddly about checkers and didn't expect to win, taking pleasure in Jack's gleeful capture of their pieces. And when they said good-bye, after tea and homemade honey buns, the tears in Jack's eyes were so genuine that they forgot their embarrassment at not understanding what he was saying, as he talked faster and faster, trying to hold them. Each one was beautiful to him, said Aunt Dodo; he fell in love at every single checker game he ever had, which is why they had to ration them severely. He was upset and moody for days afterward, mooning at his window, searching out his love among the strong-limbed, panting girls galloping back and forth across the hockey field.

But Thelma got scared, or repelled, right away, forgetting to put out her left hand as Aunt Gussie had instructed her, then wincing with pain as Jack squeezed her hand backwards.

"Jack's been typing package labels and addresses for almost eight years now," Aunt Dodo explained. "He works for a mail-order company and makes very good money." This was not entirely true, the pay was pitiful, but the sisters were proud of Jack's job and praised him for it. He was a slow typist, but faultless, a perfectionist: every address centered, every letter correct. And over the years his hands and fingers had grown strong, at least compared to the rest of his underweight and undersized body. His large pale head wavered on a stalk of a neck; beneath a high forehead his blue eyes were long-lashed and intelligent, with an upsetting ability to enlarge enormously at moments of excitement or frustration.

"Do you like chickens?" Jack asked, in a rush. When he smiled, the gold in his teeth glinted. Any other girl, said Aunt Dodo, would have known he was talking about checkers, but Thelma seemed unable to make the tiniest leap of imagination, and this in turn made Jack self-conscious and nervous. Some of the other girls had put him so at ease that he was able to talk very well; long, complicated sentences came tumbling out, only slightly garbled. At times he was so pleased with what he said that he'd have to excuse himself and go look in the mirror, tilting his head as if thinking, *So that's what I looked like when I said that!* But Thelma just looked puzzled no matter what he said, and turned helplessly toward the sisters.

Perhaps to control herself, she played checkers with grim determination and intensity, growing more and more angry as Jack marched across the board, moving very fast and without apparent thought. Although Thelma was small she had prominent breasts and Jack stared at them with obvious enjoyment. This was a trait, the sisters claimed, that he picked up from Uncle Frank who, as he headed into his sixties, would sit on the porch watching the college girls go by on their bicycles. When a particularly pretty one passed, he would stomp his feet and bang his head on the porch railing.

Thelma's face turned a deep red and it was hard to say which emotion was causing it. In the third game, when she had jumped one of Jack's pieces only to suffer a double-jump in return, she cried, "Stop looking at me like that," so startling Jack that his arm twitched, sweeping the pieces off the board, and they clattered and rolled on the parquet floor. The monkey leaped off his lap with a shriek and began scooping up the checkers with his long black clever fingers, carrying them to the top of the china closet. In the confusion Jack began to cry, his head on the table, his body wracked with convulsive sobs. Aunt Dodo wrapped her arms around him, but he only sobbed louder. Thelma jumped up, ran out of the house, and—Aunt Gussie found out later, when she returned Thelma's abandoned jacket—complained to the dean about "that madhouse" on the edge of the campus. The dean had his secretary get in touch with the proper Social Service organization, and the end result was the initial visit of Miss Pennyfeather, which had not been an unqualified success.

Miss Pennyfeather was really quite nice, though it was difficult to explain to her what Jack was doing in a house with three old ladies to whom he was not related and who had not adopted him. Wasn't he dangerous? she wanted to know; he had badly frightened Miss Freese.

"She frightened *him*," Aunt Dodo huffed. "No one has spoken to him like that since he picked up Frank's revolver five years ago!"

"What?" said Miss Pennyfeather.

Lottie's husband had been a policeman, Aunt Dodo explained, pointing to the pair of handcuffs hanging from a hook on the side of the china closet, and one time Jack had picked up Frank's service revolver. It was empty, of course, not like the time Lottie herself had picked one up, but when Jack playfully pointed it at him, Frank had walked up to the boy and slapped him across the face for his own good. Jack had cried for weeks, it seemed, but he got over it because he understood that Frank had hit him because he loved him. And no one had spoken sharply to Jack since that time.

"We think Jack understands *everything*," Aunt Dodo concluded. "He just gets it bottled up inside him."

Jack was the son of another policeman who had joined the St. Paul force about twelve years ago. Uncle Frank was the man's immediate superior and soon found out that the boy was a source of despair, financial and otherwise, for his parents. They began bringing Jack over on weekends to be watched by the three sisters, and then eventually during the week, too, where he was cared for by Aunt Dodo, the oldest, who had retired from teaching at the age of sixty-two because of a goutish leg that made standing for long periods of time impossible. Aunt Dodo had taught typing, and she continued to do what came naturally to her: she taught Jack to type, to the great amazement of his parents, though not to Frank and her sisters. "She could teach the Pope to eat pork," said Uncle Frank, who had mixed-up notions of other religions' dietary practices.

It was a perfect arrangement, emotionally and practically. At the time Aunt Dodo and Aunt Gussie, neither of whom had married, lived upstairs, and Uncle Frank and Aunt Lottie, childless, lived below. They were a passionate family, fond of music, politics, pinochle, checkers, and cribbage, not to mention the monkey Pesky, whom they had acquired when Lottie shot the organ-grinder. There had been burglaries in the neighborhood; Frank had been teaching her to use a small derringer when he was called to the phone, and the gun had gone off, according to Lottie, by some form of spontaneous combustion, shooting through the front window and wounding a passing organ-grinder named Ugo Pesti, whose name they thought to be Pesky until they saw it written down. They took him into the house for some first aid and saw him several times after that for the purpose of negotiation, the end result being a small settlement in cash and the purchase of Pesky, a stout capuchin monkey whose humorous expression and tonsured head gave him the look of a miniature Chaucerian friar.

Frank had tried to protest. "What do we want with some damned African monkey swinging through the house by his tail?" he said. "We'll all get fleas and start jibbering like Tarzan." Here he beat his chest, and the monkey, either thinking he was being called or because Frank was the only other man, jumped on his shoulder and clasped him around the neck. It was the right move to make.

The monkey sipped at, but scarcely lowered, the great reservoir of affection and energy the sisters possessed, so when Jack came into their lives he stepped into a void aching to be filled. Aunt Dodo, in particular, couldn't get enough of him and Jack throve under her constant care. He had tended to be sickly, subject to fits and other disorders, but his health improved as she increased her time with him. Conversely, when Jack moved into the spare bedroom upstairs (ostensibly so his mother could get a full-time job), his parents' marriage broke apart, as if he had been the cement that held it together. After a while they divorced and moved to another city, leaving Jack behind, though nothing much was said and no papers were ever signed: Jack was in his twenties after all . . . Not long afterward Uncle Frank died suddenly, within a week of retirement, and now, three years after that, the sisters lived on a combination of Social Security and small pensions, plus Gussie's half-time salary. "But the house is paid for," they said, seeing Miss Pennyfeather's frown, "and Jack has a steady job, too."

Miss Pennyfeather pressed her pretty lips together and shook her head, causing Jack to imitate her, which he did quite well, narrowing his eyes like someone who knows there's a mouse in the soup.

"It's not the money I'm mainly worried about, at least not yet," she said, looking at the three gray heads lined up on the couch. "We could even help you on that score." Miss Pennyfeather was sitting in the old black rocker and Jack was in his chair at the typewriter, Pesky sprawled on his lap. She began to explain, but Aunt Dodo covered her ears, so she stopped.

Aunt Lottie covered her eyes.

Aunt Gussie covered her mouth.

There was a silence while Miss Pennyfeather considered what to say. Jack broke the spell by turning red and guffawing, banging his left hand on his knee so that Pesky leaped up to the china closet.

"Get down here!" Aunt Dodo said, as the sisters lowered their hands. "Frank used to tell us it looked like three more monkeys in the house when we sat on the couch together, so we used to do that to tease him. I'm Hear No Evil." She looked around at the others for approval.

"Jack loves us to do it, so we try to do it at least once a day," said Lottie. Jack was smiling, covering his eyes with his left hand.

Miss Pennyfeather decided her best resource was her natural dignity. "What I worry about, frankly, are your ages." She hesitated. "*Is* your ages. What will happen to Jack when you're gone? He's become dependent on you. What if you get sick? It seems to me you have very little leeway for emergencies. Who would you contact?"

The sisters had no idea where Jack's parents were. The mother had gone to St. Louis, Aunt Gussie thought. "But she didn't even like Jack," she whispered as Jack typed. "She was afraid of him. She didn't think he could learn anything."

"When we taught him to play pinochle, she didn't believe us," Aunt Lottie remembered. "So we invited her over to watch. But *she* didn't know how to play pinochle herself—can you imagine?—and insisted we were just throwing cards in a pile."

"Jack was so nervous and proud he kept dropping the

cards," Aunt Dodo put in. "Frank said he was doing it on purpose to throw us off our games."

"Well," said Miss Pennyfeather, "I think we could find the parents. Maybe that's the thing to do. It seems you've done an excellent job with him"—she smiled, standing up—"and Miss Freese was just a little over-excited. We just want to do what's best for Jack, the same as you. What I'll do now—I'm just what is called a preliminary field reporter—is to make a report, and you'll be hearing from someone in the agency fairly soon. Thank you very much for the honey buns, they were delicious." As she awkwardly backed out the door, the three sisters stared at her without smiling. Jack's hands were frozen above his typewriter, and even Pesky seemed to be pointing an accusatory finger.

Mr. Mason, the man from the agency, didn't show up for almost four months, so they had almost talked themselves into believing that he was never going to come. But he came, finally, early in January when snow was banked high against the house, and the north wind shuddered against the doors and windows, so that they were sitting inside with heavy sweaters on, drinking tea and playing cards in the kitchen, which was the warmest room in the house. Jack was typing at the table set up between the dining and living rooms, wearing a long stocking cap that Pesky occasionally took a swing at. The Christmas decorations were still up. On the front door hung a lopsided circle of pine cones strung together.

"Jack did that," said Aunt Lottie, letting Mr. Mason in. A large heavyset man with a melancholy air about him, he shivered and kept his long dark coat on as the sisters settled on the couch, shifting and fluttering like birds in a nest. "He did a *lot* of the decorations." The tree had no electric lights but had clumps of tinsel, cutouts of angels and stars, bright-colored paper chains, and a few ornate, though aged, Christmas balls.

Mr. Mason had several reports: one from Jack's doctor about the high bilirubin level in Jack's blood, one from Miss Pennyfeather, and one from the agency reporting that Jack's mother had still not been found and that Jack's father didn't know where she was. *He* was a night watchman in Chicago, had remarried, and his new wife had three young children. Jack's father was happy with the situation as it was; and no wonder, said Mr. Mason.

Aunt Lottie burped. "Cucumbers and radishes always repeat on me," she said. Mr. Mason wasn't sure the sisters had been paying attention. They were waiting for the bottom line.

"What we're concerned about," he pronounced, looking at each sister in turn, "is that Jack be protected in case of emergencies. Suppose he starts having seizures again? This is always possible, with a high bilirubin count like his. And you don't even have a car. Another problem is, is he realizing all of his potential? I know," he hurried on, as the three old women stiffened as one, "that you have done wonders with him and have taught him a great deal. But we aren't quite sure how much he knows or how much he can do."

"He's good at cards," said Aunt Gussie, "and nobody can beat him at checkers! Would you like to try?"

"Chickens," blurted Jack from the typing table.

"No, no," said Mr. Mason, waving his hand. "Not now. I know how good you have been for him, but I have the feeling he would learn even more in a more"—he paused, searching—"*educational* environment."

There was a stunned silence. The sisters looked as if they had been simultaneously slapped. Jack's typewriter stopped.

"Goddamnit to hell," cried Aunt Dodo, her thin white hair flying in the draught. "How can you talk like that? If you try to take that boy you'll have to take me, too!" She stood up, lurching on her bad leg, and roughly grabbed Jack's motionless hand. While Jack's eyes bulged until they almost blew out of his head, she snatched Uncle Frank's handcuffs off the china closet and snapped them over his corded twisted wrist and her mottled brittle one. She waved the key in her other hand.

"I'll swallow the key," she shouted, her old voice cracking with fierceness. "I'm ready!"

"Go to it, Dodo," said Aunt Lottie, although the key looked entirely too large to go down without strangling her.

Mr. Mason was not an unreasonable man. He looked nervously at Jack, who was changing color every few seconds. He was thinking many things at once. One was that maybe Jack was keeping these old harridans alive and would continue to do so. Another was, well, he could always keep track by a phone call every few months. The last, somewhat ungenerous, one was, simply, if they wanted him so much, they could have him. Save the State money. He would figure something out temporarily.

"Very well then," he said, with as much formality as he could muster. "Keep working with him. I'm going to send you some forms and I'll expect a report every few weeks." Gussie got up and opened the door for him without saying anything. The icy wind ruffled the Christmas tree, the drying needles dropping off and drifting across the floor. Mr. Mason stepped out into the world.

Gussie pulled the door to and walked over to the typewriter where Aunt Dodo and Jack clustered in a state of shock. She took the key, opened the handcuffs, and hung them back on the china closet. Jack put his head against Aunt Dodo's withered breast and they stayed there, the truest lovers in the world. Aunt Lottie sat down at the spinet; it was going to be a night for singing.

"Lily robins," Jack whispered. "Goddamnit to hell."

"Listen to him," said Aunt Dodo. "Finally he gets something right."

The
Ponoes

When I was ten years old I couldn't sleep because the minute I closed my eyes the ponoes would get me. The ponoes were pale creatures about two feet tall, with pointed heads and malevolent expressions, though they never said anything. What they did was to approach me slowly, silently in order to build up my fear (because I knew what they were going to do); then they would tickle me. I was extremely ticklish in those days. In fact, I could hardly bear to be touched by any-body, and the ponoes would swarm over me like a band of drunken and sadistic uncles, tickling me till I went crazy, till I almost threw up, flinging my legs and arms around in breathless agony. I would wake up soaked, my heart banging in my chest like the bass drum in the school marching band. This lasted almost an entire year, until the Murphy brothers got rid of them for me.

Because the ponoes would come whenever I fell asleep, I hated to go to bed even more than most children. My parents were not sympathetic. Ponoes didn't seem that frightening to them, nor were they sure, for a long time, that I wasn't making them up. Even my best friend, Frankie Hanratty, a curly-haired black-eyed boy of unbounded innocence, was dubious. No one else had ever heard of them; they seemed like some sort of cross between elves and dwarfs. But where did I get the name? I think my parents felt that there was something vaguely sexual about them, and therefore dis-tasteful.

"Now no more talk about these, um, ponoes, young man. Right to bed!"

"I'm afraid!" That year—1942—I was always close to tears, and my bespectacled watery eyes must have been a discouraging sight, especially for my father, who would take me to the Dodger games at Ebbett's Field and introduce me to manly players like Cookie Lavagetto and Dixie Walker. I had a collection of signed baseballs that my father always showed to our guests.

Because I was terrified, I fought sleep with all my might. I read through most of the night, by lamplight, flashlight, even moonlight, further straining my already weak eyes. When I *did* fall asleep, from utter exhaustion, my sleep was so light that when the ponoes appeared on the horizon— approaching much like the gangs in *West Side Story,* though of course I didn't know that then—I could often wake myself up before they reached me. I can remember wrestling with my eyelids, lifting them, heavy as the iron covers of manholes we'd try to pry open in the streets, bit by bit until I could see the teepee-like designs of what I called my Indian blanket. Sometimes I would get just a glimpse of my blanket and then my eyelids would clang shut and the ponoes were upon me. It is possible, I suppose, that I only *dreamed* I was seeing my blanket, but I don't think so.

Sometimes I would give up trying to open my eyes, give up saying to myself *This is only a dream,* and turn and run. My one athletic skill was, and remains still, running. There were few who could catch me, even at ten, and today, premature white hair flying, I fill our game room with trophies for my age bracket in the 5,000- and 10,000-meter races along the eastern seaboard. Often, toward the end of a race, I hear footsteps behind me and I remember the ponoes; the adrenalin surges again, and the footsteps usually fall back. But in my dreams the ponoes would always gain and my legs would get heavier and heavier and I'd near a cliff that I would try to throw myself over, but it was like running through waist-deep water with chains on and I would be dragged down at the edge. This, I suppose, with variations and without ponoes, is a common enough dream.

My mother was more compassionate to me because at that time she too was suffering from a recurring dream. She would find herself lost in a forest, on a dark path. The ground was soft beneath her bare feet. With a vague but mounting terror she would begin to run; it soon became clear she was running on a carpet of toads and frogs. The path ended at a huge pit into which the frogs were tumbling, pouring. Whatever it was that was pursuing her approached and she screamed. Sometimes she would scream only in the dream and sometimes she would scream in actuality as well. But since her dream only came once a week, or even less frequently, she didn't have the problem with sleeping that I did. Even she would lose patience with me, mainly because my schoolwork, along with everything else, suffered. Mother was very high on education and was determined that I was going to be the first member of our family to go to college. Norman Vincent Peale preached at a nearby church and the neighborhood was awash with positive thinking.

During this year, since I scarcely slept in bed, I fell asleep everywhere else: in the car, at the movies, even at dinner, a true zombie. In the winter I liked to curl up on the floor near the silver-painted radiators, whose clanking seemed to keep the ponoes away. I would drop off at my desk at school, once clattering to the floor and breaking my glasses, like some pratfall from the Three Stooges, whom we watched every Saturday afternoon at the Quentin Theater. Eleven cents for a double feature, it was another world! But Miss McDermott was not amused and would rap my knuckles sharply with her chalkboard pointer. She was a stout and formidable old witch, and when she first came at me, aiming her stick like an assassin from *Captain Blood*, I thought she was going to poke my eyes out and leaped from my seat, to the delight of my classmates, who for weeks afterwards liked to charge at me with fingers pointed at my nose.

We had moved from the Irish section of Boston to the Irish section of Brooklyn, and my father, Little Jack Shaughnessy, liked to hang around the tough bars of Red Hook where—he told me—there was a cop on every corner looking for an Irish head to break. My father was Little Jack and I was Little Jim (or Littlejack and Littlejim) because we were both short, but he was husky, a warehouse worker at Floyd Bennett Airport. Though he was not a chronic brawler, he liked an occasional fight and was disappointed in my obvious fear of physical violence.

"Come on, Jimmy, keep the left up." He'd slap me lightly on the face, circling around me. "Straight from the shoulder now!"

I'd flail away, blinking back the tears, the world a blur without my glasses, like a watercolor painting left in the rain. To this day, when I take off my glasses I have the feeling that someone is going to hit me. Oddly enough, it was fighting that made me fall in love with the Murphy brothers, Tom and Kevin, though love may not be exactly the right word.

I was a natural-born hero-worshipper. Perhaps I still am. When I was young, most of my heroes came from books— D'Artagnan, Robin Hood—or movies, characters like the Green Hornet and Zorro, or real actors like Nelson Eddy, whose romantic scenes with Jeanette MacDonald made my classmates whoop and holler. I would whoop and holler, too, so as not to give myself away, but at night, fending off the ponoes, I would lie in bed in full Royal Canadian Mountie regalia singing, in my soaring tenor, "For I'm falling in love with someone, someone . . ." while Jeanette would stand at the foot of my bed shyly staring down at her tiny feet, or petting my noble horse, which was often in the room with us. This fantasy was particularly ludicrous as I was unable to carry a tune and had been dubbed a "listener" by Miss McDermott in front of the whole music class, after which I spent the term moving my mouth to the words without uttering a sound.

The Murphy brothers were tough, the scourge of P.S. 245. Extorters of lunch money, fistfighters, hitters of home runs during gym class, they towered over most of us because they were older, having been left back several times. Tom was the older and meaner; Kevin was stronger but slow-witted, perhaps even retarded. Tom pushed him around a lot but was careful not to get him too mad, because there was nothing that Kevin would not do when in a rage, which became increasingly evident as they grew older. Pale, lean, black-haired, they wore white shirts with the sleeves rolled up and black pants and shiny black shoes: for brawlers they were very neat dressers, early examples of the Elvis Presley look, though they never looked as soft as Elvis. Most of the rest of us wore corduroy knickers, whistling down the halls as we walked, with our garters dangling and our socks humped around our ankles. Small and weak, I wanted nothing more than to be like the two fighting brothers, who seemed to me to resemble the pictures of tough soldiers, sailors, and marines that were posted everywhere.

The Murphys had strong Brooklyn accents (they called themselves the Moifys), but the whole neighborhood was declining that way and the schools fought valiantly against it: accents were bad in 1942. I still remember the poem we all had to recite:

There was once a turtle
Whose first name was Myrtle
Swam out to the Jersey shore . . .

Tom Murphy would get up in front of the class (like many

of the others), grinning insolently, scratching obscenely, ducking spitballs, and mutter:

Aah dere wunce wuz a toitle
Whoze foist name wuz Moitle
Swam out to da Joizey shaw . . .

We would all applaud and Tom would clasp his hands above his head like a winning prizefighter and swagger back to his seat. Miss McDermott never hit the Murphys—she had wise instincts—but tried to minimize their disturbance (distoibance!) by pretending they weren't there.

But there they were: they had cigarettes, they had the playing cards with the photographs that made us queasy, they wrote on the bathroom walls and the schoolyard sidewalks. Of course, they must have written obscenities, but in the fall of 1942 they mainly wrote things like KILL THE KRAUTS and JAPS ARE JERKS: they were patriotic. I thought of the change when I visited my daughter's high school last week. Painted on the handball court was YANKEE GET OUT OF NORTH AMERICA.

And, suddenly, Tom Murphy adopted me. It was like the lion and the mouse, the prince and the pauper. Like a German submarine, he blew me out of the water and I lost all sense of judgment, which was, in 1942, a very small loss. Perhaps it was because I was so sleepy.

On rainy days when we couldn't go outside to play softball or touch football we stayed in the gym and played a vicious game the Murphys loved called dodge ball. We divided into two sides and fired a soccer-sized ball at each other until one side was eliminated. The Murphys, always on the same side, firing fast balls the length of the tiny gymnasium, would knock boys over like tin soldiers. I was usually one of the last to go as I was so small and hard to hit; no one worried about me because I was incapable of hitting anyone else, and eventually would get picked off. But one rainy September week while our marines were digging in on Guadalcanal and Rommel was sweeping across Egypt the coach had to call the game off twice in a row because the Murphys couldn't hit me before the next class started. They stood on the firing line and boomed the ball off the wall behind me while I jumped, ducked, slid in panic, like a rabbit in front of the dogs, sure that the next throw would splatter my head against the wall. Even when the coach rolled in a second ball they missed me, throwing two at a time. The truth was, I suppose, that the Murphys were not very good athletes, just bigger and stronger than the rest of us.

The next day was a Saturday, and I was out in front of our house flipping war cards with Frankie, who lived next door, when the brothers loomed above us, watching. Kevin snatched Frankie's cap and he and Tom tossed it back and forth while we crouched there, waiting, not even thinking, looking from one brother to the other. Finally Tom said, "Littlejim, go get me a licorice stick," and stuck a penny in my hand. "Fast, now, get a leg on." Mostroni's Candy Store was three blocks away, and I raced off, gasping with relief. The thought had crossed my mind that they were going to break my glasses because I had frustrated them in dodge ball. I'm sure I set an East 32nd Street record for the three-block run, returning shortly with the two sticks: two for a penny, weep for what is lost. Tom took the sticks without thanks and gave one to his brother, who had pulled the button off Frankie's new cap. Frankie still squatted there, tears in his eyes, looking at the three of us now with hatred. He could see I was on the other side. I sold Frankie down the river and waited for new orders.

"Can you get us some potatoes?"

"No," I said, "I don't think so." Tom glared at me. "Maybe one."

"Make it a big one," he said. "I feel like a mickey."

Mickeys were what we called potatoes baked in open fires. All over Flatbush you could smell the acrid aroma of charred potatoes.

"My cap," said Frankie. Kevin dropped it in a puddle from yesterday's rain and stepped on it. Ruined. Frankie picked it up, blindly, holding it with two fingers, and stumbled up the steps to his front door. We lived in a row of attached two-story brick houses, quite respectable, though sliding, with a few steps in front (on which we played stoop ball) and a handkerchief-patch of lawn, surrounded by a small hedge. In front of our house was the lamp post by which I could read at night, and next to it a slender young maple tree that my father would tie to the lamp post during strong winds.

I went through the alley to our back entrance and found my mother working in our Victory Garden of swiss chard, carrots, radishes, beets. My father went fishing in Sheepshead Bay every Saturday, a mixed blessing as he would come back loaded with fish but in a generally unstable condition so we never knew what to expect. Today I was glad, as it would make my theft easy. My mother looked up as I passed. "Littlejim, are you all right?" She has always been able to look right into my heart as if it were dangling from my nose, a gift for which I frequently wished to strangle her.

"Of course," I said with scorn in my lying voice, "I'm just thirsty."

"Well, have a nice glass of milk, sweetheart," she said, wiping her forehead and peering at me. I trotted into the kitchen and looked in the potato pail beneath the sink. There were around ten left, so I took a large one and a small one, stuck them in my shirt, and went out the front door. The Murphys were waiting down the street by the vacant lot, the fire already going.

Thus began my life of crime, which lasted almost eight months, well into 1943, for which I showed natural gifts, except temperamentally. I was always trembling but never caught. I graduated from potatoes to my mother's purse, from packs of gum at the candy store ("that Nazi wop," said Tom) to packs of cigarettes at the delicatessen: the owners watched the Murphys while my quick hands stuffed my pockets full of contraband. Under the protection of the Murphy brothers, who beat up a German boy so badly that he was hospitalized, who dropped kittens into the sewers, who slashed the tires of cars owned by parents who tried to chastise them, I collected small sums of money from boys much larger than myself. Like Mercury, god of cheats and thieves, I was the swift messenger for Tom and Kevin Murphy.

I loved them. They needed me, I thought, not reading them well. What they needed was temporary diversion, and for a while I provided that. Kevin was virtually illiterate, so, beginning with the Sunday comics one afternoon, I became his official reader. He read (looked at) nothing but comic books—*Plastic Man, Superman, Captain Marvel, The Katzenjammer Kids. Sheena, Queen of the Jungle* was his particular favorite because of her lush figure and scanty clothing.

"Get a load of that," he'd squeak (Kevin, and to a lesser extent Tom, had a high nasal whine). "What the freak is she saying?"

" 'Stand back,' " I'd read. " 'There's something in there!' "

"Freaking A!" Kevin would shout. He got terrifically excited by these stories.

It was not long before I was talking like the Murphys, in a high squeaky voice with a strong Brooklyn accent, punctuated (in school) by swear words and (at home) by half-swear words that I didn't understand. My mother was horrified.

"What the freak is this?" I'd shrill at some casserole she was placing on the table.

"Jimmy! Don't use language like that!"

"Freak? What's wrong with that?" I'd say in abysmal ignorance. "Freak, freaky, freaking. It doesn't mean *anything*. Everyone says it." This is 1943, remember.

"I don't care what everyone says," my father would shout, turning red. "You watch your lip around here, and fast!"

On weekends we sat around a fire in the vacant lot, smoking cigarettes I had stolen (the Murphys favored the Lucky Strike red bull's-eye pack, which showed through the pockets of their white shirts) and eating mickeys which I had scooped up from in front of Tietjen's Grocery. About six of us were generally there—the Murphys, myself, and two or three of the tougher kids on the block whose faces have faded from my memory.

One spring day when rains had turned the lot into trenches of red clay among the weeds and abandoned junk— people dumped old stoves, broken bicycles, useless trash there—Tom Murphy had the idea for The Lineup. This was based on a combination of dodge ball from school and firing squads from the daily news. The idea was to catch kids from the neighborhood, line them up like enemy soldiers against the garage that backed on to the lot, and fire clay balls at them. They would keep score and see who was the best shot.

"Go get Frankie and his little brother," Tom told me. To Tom, almost everyone was an enemy. "They're playing Three Steps to Germany in front of his house. Tell him you want to show him something."

Since the cap incident, Frankie had become much more alert, darting into his house whenever the Murphys appeared on the block. He often looked at me with reproach during the past months, but never said anything, and I dropped him like a red hot mickey, though he had been my only real friend.

"He won't come," I said. "He won't believe me."

"He'll believe you," Tom said. Kevin stepped on my foot and shoved me into the bushes. It was the first time he had turned on me and I couldn't believe it. I looked at Tom for help.

"Go get Frankie and Billy," he repeated. "We'll hide in the bushes."

I walked miserably down the block, sick at heart. Shouldn't I just duck into my own house? Shouldn't I tell Frankie to run? Somehow these alternatives seemed impossible. I was committed to the Murphy brothers. While my childhood went up in flames, I spoke through the blaze in my head and talked Frankie into coming to the lot for some mickeys. I was bright-eyed with innocence, knowing full well what I was doing, cutting myself off from my parents, my church, selling my friend for the love of the Murphy brothers, whom I wanted to love me back.

"My ma gave me two potatoes, they'll be ready in a couple of minutes. You and Billy can split one."

Frankie wanted to believe me. "Have you seen Tom or Kevin today?"

"They went crabbing," I said, glib with evil. "Their Uncle Jake took them out on the bay. They promised they'd bring me some blue-claws."

The walk down the block to the lot, maybe two hundred yards, was the longest I've ever taken. I babbled inanely to keep Frankie from asking questions. Billy was saved when he decided to go play inside instead—he didn't like mickeys anyway, a heresy admitted only by the very young. I didn't dare protest, for fear of making Frankie suspicious. The lot appeared empty and we were well into it before Kevin stood up from behind a gutted refrigerator; Frankie whirled around right into Tom, who twisted his thin arm and bent him to the ground.

"Lineup time!" shouted Kevin, "freaking A!" as they carried the kicking boy over to the wall. There they threw him down and tore off his shoes, making it difficult for him to run over the rusty cans, cinders, and thorny bushes. They had made a large pile of clay balls already, and the three other boys began firing them mercilessly at the cowering figure, their misses making red splotches on the garage wall. This was the first Lineup in our neighborhood, a practice that soon escalated so that within a few months boys were scaling the lethal tin cans their parents flattened to support the war effort. The Murphy boys held back momentarily, looking down at me.

"Where's Billy, you little fag?" Tom asked.

"He wouldn't come. He doesn't like mickeys." I was wincing at Frankie's cries as a clay ball would strike him.

"Maybe you ought to take his place," Tom said. "One target's not enough." Kevin reached from behind and snatched off my glasses, plunging me into the shadowy half-world in which I was always terrified. Without my glasses I could hardly speak, and I said nothing as they pushed me back and forth like a rag doll.

"You see that hoop there?" one of them said. "Bring it over to the garage and stand in it, you four-eyed freak." Squinting, I could barely make out a whitish hoop lying near the fire. I bent down and grabbed it with my right hand and went down on my knees with a piercing scream that must have scared even the Murphy brothers. They had heated the metal hoop in the fire until it was white hot and my hand stuck to it briefly, branding me for life. The older boys whooped and ran off, firing a few last shots at Frankie, Kevin not forgetting to drop my glasses in the fire, where my father found them the next day.

I knelt doubled up, retching with pain and grief while Africa was falling to the Allies and our soldiers battled through the Solomon Islands: the tide had turned. I went home and had my hand attended to—first degree burns!—and slept dreamless as a baby for the first time in years.

Conversation
with a Pole

Alcohol has always been a friend I could count on, unlike
most of my other friends. Life in the business world is no
picnic, and just when you need someone is the time they
generally pick to disappear. They transfer, and you have to
work with someone new, who has his own friends. They get
promoted or demoted. They become unavailable. But alcohol is always available, and adjustable to your needs. What
could be better than a cold beer after a set of tennis? than a
good cognac by the fireplace? It's raining outside and you
look at your lady and she smiles that special smile and
comes to sit next to you, leaning in your arms, sipping from
your glass. Or an ice-cold martini while the smell of steak is
coming from the kitchen, no, from your outside grill, and
the martini and the liver paté and stuffed mushrooms and
shrimp cocktail all go to the back of your neck and untie
that knot that seemed permanent until this very moment
and you smile thankfully and look at your guests and realize
what wonderful people they really are, and you tell them so.
Or a Bloody Mary on hung-over Sunday mornings, followed
by Eggs Benedict and a dry Chablis. I mean, isn't that what
life's all about?

When I was in business I was famous for my lunches and
dinner parties. The purchasing agents fell over themselves
trying to get invitations. They would give orders for things

they didn't want, or wouldn't need for a year, just to visit the club or get a shot at my wife's onion soup and the good Bordeaux that went with it. My two kids, bless them, were just growing up then, and they would hang around, looking like angels, emptying ashtrays and bringing out the hors d'oeuvres. I remember particularly one night old Bill McShane, the head buyer for McClintock's, and a hard man, a real hard man to please, just sat back around midnight and said, "Charlie, you win. I already told Gustafson I'd buy his stuff instead of yours, but I'll cancel the order tomorrow. This has been something else." He had downed about seven manhattans, a bottle of burgundy with dinner, and was now tapering off with brandy. Lots of people reacted that way; my wife and I would glance at each other then, surreptiously, and practically wink. It made it all worthwhile. I don't think McShane ever changed that order, though. He was one of the toughest men in the business.

I worked for Prince and Co., mainly in adhesives. It's a good field, still expanding, and Prince is the best in the field, if I do say so myself. They make compounds that will hold anything together, any combination: rubber-to-wood, paper-to-metal, plastic-to-rubber, even metal-to-metal. You wouldn't believe it would hold, but it does. Think of everything that needs some sort of adhesive compound. From one point of view, without them our entire modern world would fall apart: houses, furniture, cars, airplanes, telephones, not to mention your ordinary boxes of food and other goods. My wife has literary pretensions, she reads a lot, Book-of-the-Month and all that—she used to sneak some of the professors from our hick local college into our dinner parties, for social uplift, she said, but the poor buggers would gulp down the free drinks and puff on my cigars and pass out before dinner, so she stopped doing it. Anyway, sometimes we'd be having a little spat and I'd be sitting there, swirling a snifter of Armignac, and she'd shout, "Charlie, stop that! You're just a goddamn *glue* salesman!" And I would say, "Patricia"—never call her Pat if you value your life—"Patricia, without glue all your goddamn books would fall apart tomorrow, what do you think of that?"

But then we'd make up, and that was always fun. Patricia is a remarkable person. Like most men, I married out of a sheer lack of confidence, but I was lucky. When it was time for me to marry, I married the one who was in love with me at that time, and that was Patricia. The thought that someone else would ever fall in love with me never entered my mind. She was a lit major from Goucher College, but she still looked like the curvy blonde cheerleader she had been in high school. Her skin was so pale and smooth it was a pleasure just to run my finger over her cheekbone or down the curve of her calf just above the ankle. I was nothing but a glorified stock boy in those days. I knew I wanted to sell, and knew also I needed experience and not college to do it; but we had no idea in those good-bad old days of hamburger and cheap beer in returnable bottles that I would rise so fast in the company. In six years I had the largest territory in Connecticut and a lovely old home in Hartford; in ten years we had an elegant sloop named *Asharah* that we kept at Watch Point where we'd entertain during long sunburned weekends. Those were the days! The sloop was named after some Phoenician sea goddess that Patricia had read about, but when I painted it on I misspelled it—it should have been *Asherah*—and for a few weeks she was mad, and after me to repaint it. But after a while we got to like it: it seemed more original somehow. That's what it was like in those days: even our mistakes turned out right.

Right now the snow is coming down hard outside my window, almost like hail, and I feel a long way from Watch Point. In general, snow has a softening effect on this city, covering the dirty sidewalks, rounding the harsh corners of the apartment buildings. It brings out the kids on their sleds in a nearby vacant lot, and I like to go out and watch them, but my legs aren't what they used to be so I don't go out as much anymore. I can watch the people hurrying into Mac's grocery store or ducking into the Cloverleaf Bar for a quick beer or a game on the bowling machine. I like to lie here and smoke and think. It's comfortable. Did you ever notice how smoke rises in the air but sinks in a bottle? That's right. If you hold a cigarette in your hand the smoke rises and disperses in the upper regions (except maybe at the Cloverleaf, where the air is thicker than chowder), but if you hold a cigarette down in a bottle the smoke sinks and curls to the bottom like a net in water. Strange.

But what I wanted to tell you about was this conversation I had with a Polish engineer. It was an important conversation for me; in fact, it led to everything else that happened. Not only can I remember every word of it, I can remember, word for word, various variations that might have occurred and led to completely different conclusions. Over the past five years I have put together a series of possible conversations and followed the implications out to places far far away from Mac's grocery and the Cloverleaf Bar. One even took me to Warsaw, where I lived in the Old Town in the shadow of the castle Gorski told me about, and gave advice to the Party leaders on what adhesives to use: Gorski said they need men like me in Poland. But unfortunately the conversation didn't go that way, and I've spent a lot of time thinking about why. That's one of the pleasures of retirement: Time to think. I wish to God I had studied philosophy somewhere along the line. I often feel I'm on the verge of something really important, something about the way our lives go one way and our thoughts go another and we're caught barefoot in a no-man's-land where the ground is covered by broken stained-glass windows from old bombed-out cathedrals. That was an actual dream I had once. What it means I wish I knew.

The Piano Tuner

His name was Zbigniew Gorski—I still have his card. Despite the fact that our former National Security Advisor has the same first name, Zbigniew is tough to pronounce so everyone called him Bishek, which was funny enough. He was something less than medium height, neat, almost dapper, and curiously young-looking. I had been told he had fought with a troop of Boy Scouts in the Warsaw Uprising so I figured the youngest he could be was forty-five, a year younger than me. But I've always looked mature for my age. I was 6'2" when I was fourteen, my hair was gray by thirty-five. I think it helped me make sales, and even when I was fifteen the older boys would send me in to buy their six-packs: I had a better chance of getting served. Now I was sitting at the Blue Horse Inn with a foreigner who was my age but looked like my son.

Also, I was nervous. I usually take out directors or purchasing agents to dinner, not engineers, but this was a special case and a big order crucial to the company hinged on the outcome. Frankly, things had not been going too well for me for a year or so, and I'd been called into the office a few times to explain my decreasing sales. But the adhesive business is simply getting more competitive each year, as I explained to Roland Prince, Jr., a short stocky man with half the brains of his father despite having graduated from Wharton Business School. The father and I had been very close, and when he kicked over out on the golf course—not a bad way to go, except he fell in the water hole: for old time's sake, everyone said—I knew Prince & Co. would never be the same for me again. At any rate, at this time I wasn't the only one having trouble, sales were down all across the country, so when Bill Bishop made a huge sale to ATX Electronics involving the aircraft business and a government contract, everyone was happy because it eased the pressure across the board. But something went wrong. Their engineers told their purchasing department that our product wasn't the best one for the job. I knew it was—I had made a sale, on a much smaller scale, and it worked perfectly. That was why Prince told me to take out the engineer.

"You've done it before, Charlie," he told me. "Take him to the best place in town. Snow him. Take it easy on the booze, but snow him. This is important, Charlie. You know how to do it."

I won't say that Prince exactly threatened me, but, as I said, I was nervous. The Blue Horse is the poshest restaurant in Hartford, you practically have to wade through the carpet, and I got there a half hour early to make sure of a good table. I told them to put a couple of bottles of vodka on ice, and was on my third martini by the time Gorski came in. We hit it off right away, though he was a serious type, and I was feeling pretty good. "You're not the engineer who invented the Polish parachute?" I asked him.

"The one that opens on impact? No." He smiled slightly. I guess he had heard all the Polish jokes.

We were drinking vodka straight because that's what he had ordered: I had guessed right. Anyway, toss an olive in an ice-cold glass of vodka and what do you have? A Polish martini, and not bad either. The Blue Horse featured a Czechoslovakian beer called Pilsner Urquell, and when I suggested that as a chaser, Gorski said that was a good idea. I liked him, a man after my own heart. We got to talking about drinking habits. He always drank vodka straight, but usually here in the States the vodka wasn't served cold enough. In Poland the vodka was better, too; he drank a brand called Zytnia. I had him write it on his card because I'm interested in that sort of thing.

"You Poles are supposed to be real drinkers," I told him. "Everyone says, never try to drink with a Pole."

"We drink too much," he agreed, "but not like you Americans. We usually drink only when we eat. What did your Hemingway say? It's a way of ending the day?"

"Yes. Well, my wife would know about that," I said. "She's a great reader. I think it's a pretty good way of starting the day, too." I raised my glass and smiled at Gorski, and he smiled back. Maybe he had a sense of humor after all. But he really was stuffing in the food, skinny as he was. I wasn't too hungry myself. I was feeling light-headed, with that wonderful sense of clarity that drink can sometimes give you. Even my vision seemed sharper, and the face of the waiter as he brought us the bottles was like some old portrait where every line, every shadow, had a life and story of its own. His cheekbones alone told me he had spent a miserable childhood.

"Seriously," Gorski said, "you Americans must drink every day. You wait all day for the cocktail hour. When it comes close to that time, your face lights up and you make your martini and you sit down and say Aah! Doesn't that mean you're alcoholics?"

"We don't *have* to drink every day. We *like* to drink. It's practically a health food. We relax. It's fun."

"But you *do* drink every day!" He was beginning to get a little irritating, and I was glad to detect a slight slur in his voice. "What's the difference between having to and wanting to, as long as you do it? When was the last day you *didn't* have a drink?" he asked, and sat back like some goddamn prosecuting attorney.

I tried to think, but who keeps track of things that they *don't* do? He smiled broadly, exposing a set of very bad teeth. "If you drank more," I said, "your teeth wouldn't be so bad."

He covered them up. "You still haven't answered my question."

"I could stop anytime I wanted to," I said firmly. "In fact, I probably won't have a thing tomorrow." As I said this, I remembered we were supposed to go to the Martins' for cocktails, and for some reason this infuriated me. Suddenly it seemed hard to breathe, and Gorski's complacent face appeared to float across the table like some obscene Halloween balloon.

"You still haven't answered my question," he repeated. "When was the last day that you didn't have any drink at all?"

I suppose at that time I had been hanging by a thin emotional thread. I was tired—I hadn't slept well in weeks—and nervous, and the combination of these things with this infuriating cross-examination as if I were back in Townsend High School with its collection of vicious and sadistic teachers, all of this simply caused that thread to snap. Even so, I reacted with reasonable calm. I reached out, slowly—in actual slow motion, it seemed to me—and grabbed his tie. I pulled his head toward me, dragging his tie through that unspeakable goulash he had chosen to eat.

"Listen, you stupid Polack," I said in a low voice, "get off my back and stay off." I meant to say, "I'll drink when I want and *not* drink when I want," but I never got it out. Gorski jerked back and somehow, as I released his tie, my chair fell over backwards and I was lying on my back in the deep-piled carpet of the Blue Horse.

It was a disaster, of course. The waiter helped me up, everyone staring, and mumbled something I couldn't understand. I brushed him away, walked directly to the cloakroom, got my coat, and left the restaurant. Only when I got out in the fresh air I remembered I hadn't paid the bill, which I knew would be a whopper: the Blue Horse had fancy prices, especially on its liquor. Well, that was Gorski's problem; my problem was, we hadn't even begun to talk about adhesives.

Patricia didn't seem surprised to see me home early. She was working in the yard, which she loved to do. I poured me a whiskey, then changed my mind and dumped it in the sink. I sat by the window, looking out at our beautiful azaleas, and as usual I was disappointed. Their bloom lasts so short a time, we wait for it so long, we build up in our minds such an image of impossible beauty and fragrance that the actual imperfect presence of these fragile flowers is always anticlimactic. It is similar to what we do with our children: such energy, effort, and emotion are invested in them that we take it as a personal affront when they don't measure up to our totally imaginary and ridiculous expectations.

I was already replaying the conversation with the Pole, and worrying how I would explain it to Prince. But mainly I was thinking, Maybe Gorski was right, I shouldn't drink so much, I should get some exercise, golf or something. I really wasn't in good shape. In fact, my doctor—old Benbow, who never said you actually *had* to do anything; he was of the permissive school—had recently suggested that I cut down on drinking and smoking.

"On both of them?" I asked, winking at him. "What will you want me to cut out next?"

He didn't wink back. "I'll let you know," he said. "That'll be twenty dollars."

And I still might do it, but every time I think of starting (of stopping, rather) I think of my grandfather, old Grandpa who grew up on beer and cigars in Schweinfurt, Germany, and sustained himself on American whiskey until he was eighty-eight, working right to the end (illegally, I'm sure) as a night watchman in Bridgeport. Of course, he didn't like cigarettes. "Put out them stinkaroos," he'd tell me, passing a cigar. "Have a real smoke." He even said that to Patricia, who had innocently lit up her mentholated filtertip—the kind Grandpa hated the most—at the dinner table.

She stared at him. He stared back. Then she took the cigar, jabbed her fork through it, and proceeded to light it up in a positively Olympian cloud of smoke. There was silence around the table (except for the sucking puffing sounds Patricia was making): everyone was afraid of Grandpa. After what seemed like an hour but must have been just a minute or so, Grandpa turned to me and said, "She's all right," and everybody laughed and dinner started again and Patricia and I got married.

Gorski had got to me, all right. I went upstairs to bed without another drink (without supper, either). In the morning I told Patricia I was going to the club to play golf.

"You don't know how to play golf," she said.

"No problem," I said. "Gene Martin has played for twenty years and has never broken 100. And that reminds me, I don't feel like going to their cocktail party tonight."

She looked at me. It occurred to me that she didn't look at me very much these days. "Suit yourself," she said.

But the club was packed and I only had a vague idea of where to rent or borrow golf clubs. I soon found myself at the nineteenth hole with Archie Miller and Hank Leone. I said no to the beers, but they came anyway. I felt sad, positively sinful, as I took my first sips, but as the day wore on I gradually became angry again, just like at the Blue Horse. I could see the Pole's face leaning toward me. It was only poor overweight Archie Miller, asking what I wanted for lunch, but I felt like strangling him.

"Your trouble, Archie, is that you only think about food. That's why you look like a goddamn beach ball."

I stayed angry while I drove with Hank Leone, who had been divorced the month before and was in no happy frame of mind either, to the Martins' cocktail party. I was still in good control of myself, but when I get angry I drink faster. I was worried about the lost contract and I was worried about Patricia, back at the house. Sometimes I think I have a positive genius for suffering. I've noticed some people never seem to suffer at all, no matter what they do. Some people, even very tenderhearted ones, are entirely without conscience. I've known men and women who help strangers, love animals, cry at tragedies on TV, who think nothing of ripping off a supermarket, cheating on their income taxes or spouses, exceeding speed limits. They seem to possess no sense of guilt: these are the lucky ones. But we can't have too many of these people or our society, which is constructed almost entirely on guilt, would collapse. When the deep inner voice stops crying *Thou shalt not*, the stones will crack and grass and weeds will reclaim the streets.

In the middle of the party Roland Prince, Jr., arrived with his long-nosed wife. I saw right away that he had heard about my lunch with Bishek Gorski. He avoided me for a while, but when I went up to him he said he would like to see me in his office on Monday.

"You can talk to me now," I said, "if you're not afraid to speak (I nodded at his wife) in front of Cyrano here."

"You're fired, Charlie," he said.

"Listen, shrimpboat," I said, "let's step outside and see who can fire whom." I knew as I said this it didn't make much sense, but I was past caring by now. Hank Leone somehow steered us apart, and later on in the evening Patricia came to pick me up. I was lying on a big pile of coats in the guest room. The next morning I got up, hitchhiked to the club, picked up my car, and started driving west.

That was five years ago. I had the vague idea of going away, drying up, starting over. I kept going till I came to this sleepy Midwestern city with its pink motels and cheap flophouses and free lunches. Small checks follow me, and I'm reasonably contented. Now that I'm over fifty, I don't have the energy I used to have. I could write the kids, but somehow even that seems too hard to do. Once in a while, when a check comes, I splurge on a bottle of Martell's Cordon Bleu and share it with the gang here. They don't even know what it is. We sit around on our bunks drinking it out of paper cups, hiding them when Mrs. Matthews comes in to check on us. I get a kick out of that. And sometimes I exercise my old skills, just to show off. The Cloverleaf is going to raffle off a station wagon and the one who sells the most tickets gets a free Christmas turkey. I've already sold so many we're planning on a great feast.

But mainly I pick up bottles of this cheap and perfectly palatable wine. I lie here in the twilight and think. I blow smoke in a bottle and watch it sink. Hey. That rhymes. Patricia would be proud of me.

Losers
Pay

I met him first on the basketball court. He was one of those small awkward players who throw themselves into basketball with tremendous energy, waving their arms, running erratically from man to man, never grasping the pattern of the game. Though he irritated me to the point where I would stop playing and hold the ball while he leaped around me, slapping my arms, the six of us (playing three-on-three) went out afterwards for beer—losers pay—and our friendship began that afternoon.

I liked him for perverse reasons, which is why I like most of my friends. Though he was a freshman and I a junior, he was loud and opinionated. "The fucking dean hasn't read a book in fifteen years," he would say, or, "The whole goddamn lit department are fags." And I would defend the dean, who was a nice guy, and the lit professors, who were very serious men; but while I was telling Curtis how unreasonable his attacks were, I was thinking how he had the feel for certain symbolic, if not literal, truths.

Perhaps his background qualified him for this, because it was so dramatic, so excessive. Curtis Ganz was the only one at our school whose father had been murdered, though Ev Colson's dad had driven off the Skyway Bridge in a 1969 Buick under strange circumstances. But to have a father murdered, that was something, and many of us developed a definite loathing for our sedentary parents doomed to die slowly of overweight and cigarettes. Curtis's father, he told

us, had been a flamboyant lawyer, and one night was arguing
a case in the local bar when his opponent drew a small pistol
from his pocket and shot him through the nose, bringing Mr.
Ganz to a bloody and reasonably painless end, as he never
recovered consciousness.

This had happened over ten years before, when Curtis was
only eight or nine, and the murderer had already served his
time and was paroled on good behavior. He, the murderer,
was doing fine, but the Ganz family had never recovered, the
children scattered to relatives, Mrs. Ganz having long been a
semi-invalid. For a lawyer, Curtis's father had turned out to
be dazzlingly unprepared for sudden death: no life insurance, no will, no mortgage insurance. By the time Curtis got
to college he was pretty much on his own, earning his own
money, choosing Monroe College because it gave him the
largest scholarship.

Curtis was going to major in law. His ambition was to be a
tough prosecuting attorney or a "hanging judge." "I want to
see those fuckers swing," he would tell us, giving us his juve-
nile-delinquent stare. Curtis had barely begun to shave and
still looked more like a high school sophomore than a college freshman.

Our teachers both loved and feared him, because he was so
cantankerous in class. In the long stretches of dull after-
noons while the radiators and professors rattled on inter-
minably, Curtis's classes had a certain edge to them. Everyone would be gazing out the windows at the leaves whirling
through the quadrangle or listening to the wind shaking the
ancient windows of Truax Hall when Curtis would stand up
and say, "Sir, why do all our major writers hate the Jews so
much?" (Half of our class was Jewish.)

"Well, they don't really, Curtis," the professor would begin. We had been reading Eliot and Pound and were now in
the midst of *The Sun Also Rises*. "There are some anti-
Semitic references in their work, but perhaps this is just a

reflection of the anti-Semitism found in our society at the time."

"They're not just references," Curtis would say, and proceed to quote nasty anti-Jewish excerpts: he always did his homework. And the class would be off on a raging debate on the relation of morality to art, or, as Curtis liked to phrase it, of stupidity to talent. His general position seemed to be that most of our writers had their heads up their asses and were enjoying the view.

In the evenings we would go down the hill to the local bars where we would play the bowling machines; losers would pay for a beer and the next game. Curtis was a fanatical player and an almost continual loser, though occasionally he had a sensational game, unrolling strike after strike so that often his name was chalked up on the board as the high game of the month even while he was losing 90 percent of the time. He also would get into fights with the "townies" because of his constant needling of the opposition. "Your turn, fatso," he would say to a 200-pound metalcaster from the local foundry. Of course he never won his fights, but then he wouldn't officially lose them either, as he never gave up: we would have to pry his opponent off him and carry Curtis, kicking and cursing, out to the streets. We believed he would have to be killed or beaten absolutely senseless before he would stop fighting.

On quiet nights we sat around and talked about what we would do when we finished school. I was going to be a poet. "Write for TV, you twit," Curtis would say. "At least that would be useful." Curtis viewed TV as the opiate of the masses. The best thing you could do for the American people was to give them something inane to stare at while they sucked their thumbs; this kept them from beating their children or burning down the First National Bank. Though he didn't have anything against beating children. "Children are always a projection of their parents," he would announce.

"Therefore child abuse is the equivalent of self-abuse, and hence pleasurable. The little pricks." We loved to hear him talk like this; it was like having a profane and adolescent Samuel Johnson in residence.

But the subject he would talk about most often was his father, and his father's death. He had been a wonderful father. Before he was murdered they lived in the best house in Schenectady. All the fat G.E. bigwigs jostled their pink behinds to get invited to their parties. They had a spiral staircase, a tennis court, a bar stocked with every intoxicating beverage the fuckers have invented. And all that was lost because a little cross-eyed runt named Albert McGinnis put a bullet through Mr. Ganz's nose in an after-hours bar called The Corporal.

What's more, the story was perfectly true. Because of Curtis's conversational mixture of diatribe and outrageous exaggeration, there were those of us who were skeptical of anything he said, so I checked it out. I went downtown to the office of the Schenectady *Dispatch*, feeling guilty as I did so, and went through the yellowing papers of a decade ago. It didn't take me long to find it, a brief article tucked away on the second page of the city section:

Schenectady Lawyer Murdered. Albert McGinnis, 57, of 227-1/2 Maple St., has been charged with second-degree murder in the shooting death of Murray Ganz, 35, a lawyer associated with the firm of Miller, Pack & Henry, following an argument in a local tavern.

There was another paragraph or two, but I couldn't find anything about the trial or the sentencing, or about McGinnis's eventual release. Still, it proved Curtis's story was not the product of a fevered imagination, however he might have embellished it.

One night, very drunk, Curtis stated flatly, "I'm going to

shoot the bastard. Some day I'm going to find him and shoot him in the stomach and talk to him so he knows who did it. And I'll do it so I'm not caught. Anybody can murder anyone and get away with it in this dumb fucking country."

"No you can't," I said. "That's stupid."

"I'll do it slowly," Curtis said. "I'll burn his house down first. I'll haunt him for a year." He had it all planned out, he had been thinking about this for a long time. Suddenly it seemed that he could think of nothing else; in the next few weeks he dwelt on it incessantly, building baroque fantasies of assassination and torture. Nothing we could say could dissuade him, and to tell the truth we didn't try very hard. It was exciting, and there seemed to be some justice in it. A tale of murder and revenge. Being involved in this was more interesting than Biology 102 or third-year French, and so we were sucked into his movie, as the saying goes.

The first problem, which we never really expected to solve, was to locate the murderer. There was no Albert McGinnis in the telephone directory. We soon hit on the idea of going down to The Corporal, to "make inquiries," Sam Spade-style. To combine drinking with detective work seemed to us the perfect activity. The Corporal was a grungy little bar in what we thought of as the Polack section of town. Strange meats (pig knuckles?) and huge pickles floated obscenely in jars on the counter-tops, polka music twanged from the jukebox, a dirty pool table crowded the far corner. A sign on the mirror said: Three Reasons for Making Love to Women Over 40: They don't swell / They don't tell / And they're GRATEFUL as hell.

There were four of us: Ev Colson, Marv Bluestein, Curtis, and myself. We sat at a filthy table with our beers. Colson said, "Jesus, you can get crabs just sitting here. And Polack crabs are bigger than blue-claws." We picked out the oldest people in the bar as the best bets for knowing anything about McGinnis. I was assigned a gray-haired man with a large beerbelly and tattoos on both muscular arms. He was sitting at the end of the bar, and after gulping down my beer for courage I moved next to him and ordered two more. The man took his without saying anything.

He was difficult to talk to and I knew why. I smelled of college. Curtis once said that college boys all smell alike to the working class—a repellent mixture of soap and fear, maybe, because we were scared shitless when we were talking to them. But gradually, as I bought more beers, he began answering my questions. Yeah, he was a regular customer, he'd been coming here a long time. Yeah, for more than ten years, you could fill a fucking battleship with the beer he'd knocked off here. And finally, no, he didn't know no McGinnis. Oh, that guy, the one who knocked off that asshole lawyer. Whaddaya want to see him for? Nah, he never comes here anymore, not for years, he's a night watchman or something somewhere. Nah, I don't know where, how about another beer, all right?

We had arranged to meet at Tony's, another bar down the street, when our conversations had finished—we were trying to avoid looking conspiratorial. When I got there Ev Colson was sitting alone at a table. "Jesus," he said, "I'm no good at this. I was through in thirty seconds. Nothing."

"McGinnis is a night watchman somewhere," I told him, and we settled down to wait for the others. Curtis was next in, with no information. "The fucker didn't even know his own name," he said, drinking my beer.

But Bluestein came in with an excited look. "Got it," he crowed, so we had to shush him down. "McGinnis is a night watchman!"

"We already know that, peabrain," said Curtis. Bluestein looked deflated.

"But we don't know where," I said.

"Ah! Well, I do." He leaned forward. "McGinnis is a night watchman at Thornton Plastics out on Old Woodbridge

Road. And he has breakfast at the Red Dragon five mornings a week. This guy I talked to knows because he met him there and tried to get him to smuggle out a carton of dishes." Bluestein looked at us triumphantly. "But he wouldn't," he added.

"Wouldn't what?" asked Colson.

"Wouldn't smuggle out the dishes. Are you listening, cretin?"

The next few days jumped by nervously. To our surprise, we had found with little trouble the murderer of our friend's father. Now it was up to Curtis. On Thursday he said, "To-morrow let's find out where he lives, trace him from Thorn-ton's to his house."

Old Woodbridge Road ran just outside the city. The Thorn-ton Company was a small factory specializing in plastic dishes for diners and schools. Only one light was burning there, in a small room near the main entrance. We arrived around four in the morning, parked by the side of the road, and sat smoking in silence in Colson's new Pontiac. A finger-nail moon hung over the factory smokestack, balancing for a while like a Steinberg cartoon; below it, shining in the soft light, an old-model Chevy stood alone in the parking lot.

A little before six, other cars began to arrive and by the time the old Chevy started up the parking lot was fairly crowded, so much so that from our vantage point none of us saw the driver get in. Letting the Chevy get a little lead, Colson swung his car in a U-turn and followed about a hun-dred yards behind. It was still dark, we couldn't see each other's faces, and somehow this kept us quiet.

"He's going to the Red Dragon, all right." Bluestein broke the silence.

The Red Dragon was an all-night diner, near the railroad tracks and familiar to all of us. From 11:00 P.M. to 2:00 A.M. it was a combination college and gay hangout, but by break-fast time it was filled with the early risers—factory workers, secretaries, sleepy policemen stirring their coffee. We decided that Bluestein and I would go into the diner with McGinnis, leaving Curtis and Colson in the car to make sure we wouldn't lose him.

The eastward stars were winking out as we followed McGinnis's huddled figure into the Red Dragon. He sat at the counter and we took a table behind and to the right of him. The first thing we noticed was his white hair. He was an old man! We hadn't thought about that. Of course, he must be almost seventy by now! We watched him eat. He was small, wiry, unkempt, hunched over his breakfast in a ragged corduroy windbreaker, shoveling in the food, eyes fixed on the plate so it was hard for us to see his face, except that he wore glasses.

"Christ, he wears glasses," said Bluestein, as if that changed something. "He looks like that crazy scientist in Captain Marvel."

"Or like Einstein."

"It's the same thing. Hey, let's go." McGinnis had gone to the cashier, and we stood behind him to pay for our coffee. He was even smaller than I had thought. I could have put my hand on his shoulder; in fact, I had a terrible urge to do so. I would say, "Al, baby, you don't know us, but we have a friend outside who is the son of the man you shot through the nose. He's going to make you pay for that, old man."

While this was whirling through my brain McGinnis collected his change, turned, and looked directly at me. His light blue eyes were bloodshot, his old face pale and unhealthy-looking. Though he looked at me just for a moment and without expression, my stomach lurched and I felt my face flushing furiously, then draining equally fast.

We hurried out to the car.

"He's an *old* son-of-a-bitch," said Bluestein, as Colson began following the Chevy once more. Curtis was silent, staring ahead as McGinnis wound through the less prosperous neighborhoods of Schenectady until we arrived, in a brief time, at one of those trailer parks that blot our landscape: not a tree, not a curved line, to soften the effect of three hundred more or less permanent hunks of tin lined up like so many cans of cat food in the A & P.

McGinnis lived toward the back of the park, the last one in the second row, and parked his car in the field behind it. We watched from a distance as he shuffled into his trailer, which looked like a miniature Red Dragon diner; then we turned around and headed back to Monroe. It's hard to say what we were thinking. We *weren't* thinking. We were waiting for Curtis to do something.

Sunday afternoon he came into the room I shared with Colson. "Lock the door," he told me. After I locked it, he looked at us for a minute, then pulled a small pistol from his pocket and placed it on my desk. "It's my father's. Tonight's the night, fellow assassins," he said.

Colson and I stared at the gun. It was black and snub-nosed; it took over the desk like a tank in the desert. "Jesus," said Colson. "You don't need that. The old fart is going to die of old age next week."

"Listen, chickenshits, that's not your worry. Anyway, we won't use it tonight. Tonight we just begin the operation."

We were chickenshits all right, but we weren't about to back out. Curtis had energy and moral force, which may be the same thing, on his side: what *should* you do when you meet your father's murderer? We were ready. We had read *Electra*.

And so, shortly before midnight on a star-studded Sunday night we set out for the trailer park and McGinnis. We wore sneakers and old clothes; we almost blacked our faces but decided against it: we weren't fucking commandos, after all. Parking just off the main road, we skirted around the park on foot, turning the corner just below McGinnis's trailer. The old Chevy was there, meaning he wasn't at work; and his home, if that's the right word for those tin boxes, was one of the very few with lights on. The car was hidden from the trailer by a thick stand of punk trees whose papery bark glowed ghostlike in the night air.

"That's good," said Curtis. "That's just right. Now we can see in but he can't see out. First, we take the car." We left Colson as a lookout at the corner of the first row, and the three of us padded up to the Chevy. It was a two-door coupe, very neat and carefully polished.

Each of us had brought a knife. For a few moments we stood motionless by the car; then Curtis knelt down and plunged his knife into the right front tire. The hiss of air seemed terrible in the darkness.

"C'mon, let's go," he whispered. The car wasn't locked and I opened the door and leaned in. The worn, cheap material gave off a faint glimmer in the starlight. Methodically I cut the seat apart, slicing first the backrest, then the seat itself, until it all hung in shreds. I threw the batting over the dashboard and into the rear of the car; then I reached over the seat and began ripping up the back, but the car squeaked and I quickly backed out. Bluestein and Curtis had slashed the rest of the tires, and the old Chevy sat on its rims. I imagined I could hear it sighing, and a phrase came to me from our reading: *And it gave up the ghost.*

Curtis motioned. "Now the house." We followed him to the trailer and flattened ourselves against the metal siding by the front window where the light was pouring out on the bare hard dirt of the park.

"Suppose he sees us?" Bluestein's face was chalk white.

Curtis looked at him and patted the bulging pocket of his pea jacket: he had brought the pistol. There was nothing to say, not now.

Running beneath the long front window was a homemade window box painted green, maybe four feet long. In it were growing ten or twelve young geranium plants, a pathetic attempt to bring something living and natural into that metallic graveyard. Curtis ducked under it and ran to the other side of the window; he began pulling out the geraniums, ripping them apart as he did so. Bluestein and I followed suit, crouching below the box, reaching up and tearing the flowers out.

Only when the window box was empty did we look inside, into the living room. Sitting in a wheelchair, profile to us, an old woman was watching TV. She was heavy, but not unattractive, like a German grandma. There was something wrong with one of her legs, which was enormous. So McGinnis had a wife, or a woman at any rate. Who would have thought? We watched her, as hypnotized by her presence as she was by the TV.

After a while McGinnis came in behind her. She didn't see him; he didn't see us. He stood there behind her chair, a little old man in pajamas. Then he put both hands on her shoulders. She didn't turn around, but lay her head to the side on one of his hands; the other he slipped inside her bathrobe and rested on her breast. They stayed there, without speaking, for a long time, his white head motionless above hers, both watching television. We watched, too, frozen by a scene beyond our experience.

"FREEZE! DON'T MOVE!"

My heart slammed like a fist as a white light hit us and we were looking at a very large policeman with his hand on his holster. "Don't move, don't one of you move!" He came closer, peering over the flashlight.

"All right, what're you boys up to? Peeping Toms or what? What's all this?" His flashlight picked up the pile of shredded geraniums.

"We're from the college, sir," I said, barely able to breathe. "We were just fooling around. I don't know why we did it."

The front door opened. McGinnis stood in the doorway,

squinting toward the disturbance. He began walking toward us.

"Sorry, Mr. McGinnis," said the policeman. "These boys were looking in your window. They say they're from the college, and it looks like they've been doing some damage."

McGinnis stared down at the geraniums and then at us. "What d'you want to do that for?" he asked in a quavering voice. "My wife was crazy about them flowers. She ain't got nothing she loves like them flowers. That's all she had in this dump to make her happy."

"I don't know why we did it, sir," I repeated. "We're really sorry. It was just crazy." I looked at Bluestein and Curtis. Bluestein could hardly stand up; Curtis leaned stiffly against the side of the trailer. The bulge in his side pocket looked huge.

"Do you want to press charges, Mr. McGinnis? I'd just as soon throw the book at these punks."

McGinnis came almost nose to nose with us. He didn't have his glasses on. He looked at each one of us for a long time, expressionless, and I couldn't tell if he remembered me from the Red Dragon or not. He looked at Curtis last.

"What's your name, young man?"

Curtis hesitated. "Murray," he said. Murray was his middle name, his father's name.

"Ah," said McGinnis. He looked broken all of a sudden, his energy gone, a worn-out old man. "No, no, what good would that do? I don't want to press charges. I just want some peace, please go away." He walked toward the front door. "But I don't know how I'll tell my wife about them geraniums." And he was gone.

"How'd you guys get here?" the policeman asked.

"We have a car down the road."

"All right, get the hell out of here. And if I catch you around here again I'll run you in for sure, you get that?"

"Yes sir," I said, "we're sorry." The three of us hurried away.

Colson was waiting in the car. He had seen the whole thing, but was unable to get ahead of the policeman to warn us. We got in and drove off toward the college.

"Jesus," Colson said, "wait'll he finds out about the car. You better get rid of that gun."

All this time Curtis hadn't said a word. When he finally spoke, it was in a soft voice we were not familiar with. "Did you see the way the fucker grabbed her tit? At his age!"

As we neared the college the motor began to cough: we were out of gas. We had to walk up the hill in the dark, single file, and we were grateful for that.

Even Crazy
Old Barmaids
Need Love

It takes about six months to make a decent bar. When Phil
Masters bought The Grouper he threw out the new jukebox
with its rock songs and put in the old one of his father's with
its mixture of golden oldies and country. He put in more
lights and took out some tables. He kept the stuffed fish
above the bar—an immense fat grouper with an expression
of open-mouthed wild-eyed surprise—but got rid of all the
little black-and-white photos of the previous owner and his
cronies holding up various fish between them. He brought
along a reasonably honest bartender named Harry Kee and
he kept the old barmaid, a tough-talking lady named Agnes
Prokop who had been there for six years and knew what was
what.

Phil needed Agnes because The Grouper was a tough bar
in downtown St. Petersburg. This is not very tough, because
St. Pete is a gentle town where old folks sit behind the polished counters dissolving their Social Security checks and
trying to figure out what hit them. But there are bikers and
hookers, as in any self-respecting city, and these had been
breaking furniture for about two years in The Grouper,
which is why Phil could buy it so cheaply. This wasn't his
first tough bar and he knew what to do.

The bikers came in in ones and twos, and at the first
sound they made Phil and Harry had them by the elbows and

were carrying them out. Between them, Phil and Harry weighed almost five hundred pounds and Harry in particular had a smile that would make a dog faint. "You come back here, friend, and I'll be on you like white on rice," he'd say, smiling, bumping the biker against the doorjamb with his belly. Harry's belly was a boulder not to be brushed aside lightly. Harry was about forty years old and a casebook example of grizzled. He never looked shaved and never grew a beard, but was somehow able to keep a steady four-day stubble: he looked like he had just emerged from some dark alley and was daring you to ask what he had been doing there. No one asked.

Agnes pointed out the hookers for them, at least the aggressive ones, and they too were firmly though gently escorted out. Some of the quieter ones she didn't identify. Hookers need a beer now and then like anybody else. This interest in cleaning up The Grouper was not moral but financial: a decent family bar was easier and more profitable than a white-knuckle dive. It took half a year and a lot of energy to do it. The turning point came after about two months and was, oddly enough, one of their easiest times. The bikers came back in a group; outside The Grouper their bikes revved and coughed as they gathered—a sound that should have attracted all of the town's policemen, but instead seemed to disperse them—and after a while they banged the door open and came in. Phil didn't even wait for them to get near the bar. He fired his shotgun in front of them with a blast that made several people think they were dead. For a few minutes afterwards the remaining fish pictures swung on their hooks, glass fragments dripping like icicles in the silence. As the bikers hustled back to their bikes, Harry admired the holes in the wall. "Nice pattern," he said. They were going to panel the wall anyway.

So fishermen came there, some reporters from the *Times*, college kids from the local branch of USF. Agnes made good sandwiches. A new theater opened nearby and brought them a lot of business: the theatergoers would come in before the play, and the actors would come in after it, starving for corned beef on rye and a cold pitcher of beer.

One of the regulars was a middle-aged actor named Daryl Dana, a melancholy man with a deep voice and a face like a deserted battlefield, mined with smallpox scars and three long gashes above his eyebrows. When drinking he would talk of how he had been driving with his fiancée, the only girl he had ever known who could look at him without pity or worse. He was a crazy driver, he said, and missed a turn from too much speed: they slammed through some small trees, crashed down a gully, up an embankment, and came to rest on railroad tracks parallel to the road. Both Daryl and his girl had smashed the windshield as their heads snapped back and forth, but the girl was in worse shape, cuts all over her face, blood running down her neck. They got out of the car, heard a train in the distance, and Daryl panicked. "Push the car!" he screamed. "Goddamnit, help me push the car!" The girl had sat down by the bank, and now rolled over on her side. Daryl ran to her in a frenzy, yanked her up, and dragged her to the car, where she just fell on her knees behind the rear bumper as the train rounded the bend.

"She never forgave me for that," he'd say, staring into his beer. "The train stopped in plenty of time, and suddenly there were policemen and everything around. I was pretty lucky. I was still in uniform then and the cop in charge was a patriotic bastard and didn't press charges. And my girl could have sued me to death—her face was really a mess—but she just said, 'Go away, Daryl, don't come near me anymore.' She couldn't forgive me for trying to make her push my stupid car."

His favorite audience for this morose tale was Agnes, who would listen with great concentration while he talked, as if she had trouble understanding the language. Agnes was a good-sized woman in her mid-forties, a little thick at the waist, but slim-ankled and large-bosomed. She wore her black hair in a neat bun, and her dresses were always dark, long, and severe. She often wore a green sweater pushed up to her elbows as she polished the bar or made sandwiches.

No one knew much about Agnes. Her face was unlined, but dark circles beneath her large brown eyes gave her a tragic appearance that the actors kidded her about. Charlie Robertson, the director, was always after her to join the theater group. "Come play Lady Macbeth for us! You'd be perfect!"

"I am no lady," she'd say. "I am a barmaid." Agnes had virtually no accent despite having grown up in Poland, outside of Krakow, but she somehow never learned to speak informally, in contractions. "This is The Grouper Bar speaking," she would say, answering the telephone, clearly enunciating the *ing*. Everyone else just barked, "Grouper."

What she seemed to have in common with Daryl was the fact that neither of them ever smiled. Even after she went home with him—to his room in the elegantly run-down Michigan Hotel—they were as serious as ever the next day. Everyone was curious: there are few secrets in a bar-and-acting community. Rick Seifer, one of the young leading actors who also lived at the Michigan, claimed to have heard enthusiastic cries in a foreign language, but he was not a reliable witness: he would say anything to upstage anybody.

It would not be right to call these two veterans derelicts—they both had steady jobs, after all, and bothered no one—but their companionship struck chords of compassion in various hard-nosed people. Harry posted a placard on the mirror: EVEN CRAZY OLD BARMAIDS NEED LOVE. And Phil would mutter as the crowd thinned in the early morning, "Better go sit with Creepo, I'll watch the bar." Which was as romantic as those large gentlemen ever got.

Daryl would always sit at the corner table near the poolroom, where he could hear the conversation in both rooms. He seldom took off his battered old black cowboy hat with a small iron eagle pinned to it. Stretching out his scuffed black boots, he looked like an emaciated trucker on the last leg of a transcontinental haul.

"Jesus, you look awful," Seifer would say. Seifer was always doing isometrics and ate lots of fiber.

"I like to look awful. I'm *supposed* to look awful, those are the parts I play."

"You don't have to play it offstage. And you don't have to look *dead*. Why don't you come jogging with me tomorrow morning? We'll fix you up."

"Jogging's the sport of the last resort," Daryl said, "and I'm not there yet. It's more faddish than Zen or yogurt." Agnes brought him a beer and stood by the table.

"You look like an old man," said Seifer. "Pretty soon you won't be able to play anything but grandfather parts. Jogging will knock ten years off your body. What's the matter? Afraid you can't do it?"

"All it takes to be a jogger," Daryl said to Agnes, "is a certain amount of stubbornness and meanness of spirit. No talent, no grace. Just an overwhelming fear of death."

Seifer had the infuriating habit of never getting insulted. "All right," he said, walking away, "but when you start choking to death on one of those weeds just come to me and I'll help you out, if it's not too late."

"Of course he's right," Daryl said when Agnes sat down. "I'm in terrible shape. I used to be pretty good at baseball when I was a kid. But I never thought I'd live so long. When I was a kid I couldn't imagine living to be thirty, and here I am forty-six, and still kicking, more or less." He took a deep swallow of beer.

"Why not?" said Agnes. "There is nothing wrong with you."

"I'm sick in the head, Agnieska," he said, tapping his pale scarred forehead. "El Sicko, that's me." Daryl had begun call-

75

ing Agnes by her Polish name, insisting it was far lovelier
and more feminine than the American equivalent. "I have
this terrible fear that some day, when I'm dying, I'll burst
into uncontrollable tears and cry the last twenty-four hours
of my life. Me, who's always so cheerful!"

Agnes didn't laugh; she never laughed. "You have nothing
to cry about," she said. "You want to cry, I will tell you Polish stories, then we can both cry."

"No Polish stories, I couldn't stand it. I know enough stories already. In Argentina," he said, "you know what they
do? They cut off the hands of little girls and send them in
shoe boxes to their mothers. Shoe boxes!"

"Argentina," said Agnes. "What do you know about Argentina?"

"Argentina is right around the corner."

For Daryl, everything was right around the corner: cancer,
unemployment, detached retinas, car trouble. It was just a
matter of time before these things would get you. "It's all
psychosomatic," Seifer told him. "It's in your head. *Think*
healthy and you'll *be* healthy."

"You make me feel like throwing up," Daryl said. "Did
you see all those dead fish floating in Lake Maggiore? Big
swollen bellies? El stinko? I suppose they were worried
about inflation and just keeled over."

"Fish aren't people."

"Jesus, a college education and he's just figured out that
fish aren't people." Daryl was tough on everybody, but college students brought out his most aggressive instincts. He
was always trying to drink them under the table, never
seeming to recognize that at least half of them were better
drinkers who would still be going strong while Agnes was
guiding him back to his room. He could get along with
Agnes. She had an expression—a shadow in her eye, something in her voice—that blunted his bitterness.

"Why do you put up with me?" he asked her, after she

steered him to his bed and took off his shoes. She didn't answer at first so he repeated it.

Agnes sat down on the bed. "Maybe you remind me of someone," she said.

"Tell me."

"No, I can't talk about it. I'll just say I knew a man in Poland who was as unhappy as you, but his reasons were mostly political."

"What happened?"

"They got him finally. I didn't help him enough, I was too frightened."

"Do I look like him?"

"Not really." Agnes pulled Daryl's head to her breast and began singing softly in Polish. "*Sto lat, sto lat/Niech zyje, zyje nam . . .*" Her singing voice was surprisingly pure, high, and fragile.

"What does that mean?"

"That means I want you to live for a hundred years."

"What a frightening thought! I'd have to play Methuselah!"

"Or Solomon!"

"Or Grandma Moses!"

In October a new play opened, Mamet's *American Buffalo*, and Daryl had his biggest part since he had been with the company. He played an aging small-time crook. The play attracted very small audiences—it was much too obscene for St. Petersburg—but there was general agreement that Daryl's performance was first-rate. At the same time many claimed, with Robertson, that this was because Daryl really *was* an aging small-time crook. What did any of them know about him, after all? Five years before, they had been a struggling acting company in need of an older player who would work for peanuts, and this man with the unlikely name of Daryl Dana had shown up and gotten the job without much competition and with fewer questions.

But *American Buffalo* was his time of triumph and on the

last night of the play the director gave a party in Daryl's honor. It began in The Grouper with many pitchers of beer, songs, dances, and finally toasts. "A toast to Agnes!" Charlie Robertson's face was flushed. "To the True Muse of the Central Avenue Theater, whose golden gifts"—he raised his beer—"sustain us through the dark night of the soul, not to mention all the idiotic reviews."

Everyone laughed and applauded, except Daryl. He was approaching the edge of real drunkenness. "Don't patronize Agnes," he said.

"I'm not patronizing her," said Robertson, smiling at everyone, waving his arms about. "We all love Agnes."

"You're a pompous ass, Robertson." Daryl leaned across the table on his elbows and emptied his beer on Robertson's lap. "Have a beer on me, pompous ass," he muttered, straightening up.

The director was a large man, just turning paunchy, with heavy arms and shoulders. He was feared for his quick temper—once, in a rage, he had destroyed the entire set of *Man and Superman* the night before the opening—but on this occasion he turned pale and stood up quietly. "Dana, you're a spoiled and sorrowful bastard, and I bet you ain't been spanked in forty years." The more angry Robertson was, the more Southern and ungrammatical his speech became. He began walking carefully around the table. "I'm gonna pluck you like a chicken, so you might as well jus' start layin' eggs."

Daryl hesitated for a moment; then, as the larger man approached, he jumped up, upsetting his chair, and ran to the door of the bar. "I quit," he yelled, his normally low voice pitched high and reedy, as if his throat had dried up. "I quit this two-bit outfit!" He backed up as Robertson came toward him, turned, and ran out the door onto Central Avenue.

No one spoke in the bar. It was like the frozen tableau at the end of *The Inspector General*. Several of the actors were holding their mugs of beer in the air, waiting for someone to break the spell. Agnes was the first to move: she took off her apron. She looked hard at Robertson for a moment and then went out into the night. The stars were so low they looked like airplane lights, but there was no moon in sight. She could see Daryl's hunched figure across the street, heading toward the center of town. He didn't acknowledge her cries, and it took her several minutes to catch up with him.

"Go away," he said. "I want to be alone." But then he stopped. "Jesus, I sound like Greta Garbo!"

"Daryl, it is all right. I want to be with you."

He stared at her, the emotional effort seeming to sober him. "Agnieska, go away. Can't you see I'm a clown, and a cowardly clown at that? To think I ran away from that fat-ass Robertson!"

"You are not a coward! Who wants to brawl in a bar? Phil and Harry spent a year getting rid of all the troublemakers— you did the right thing. I hate bullies like Robertson!"

By this time they were near Howard Street and the center of town; it was almost 2:00 A.M. In the entire city there were maybe a dozen people on the streets, wondering what they were doing there, or maybe past wondering. The low buildings looked beat and shabby: this was where Jack Kerouac came to die. As Daryl and Agnes walked, an occasional figure, usually black, would detach itself from the shadows and approach them, only to stop and fade back into the darkness when confronted by their self-absorption.

Around a corner, somewhat isolated from the other buildings, was Poochie's Diner, an all-night coffeehouse of indifferent cleanliness where the late nighters could meet the early risers. Poochie made good coffee, though everything else he sold seemed on the slippery side. He was a short round man with a desperate look, whose hair stood up as if constantly electrified; his only son had disappeared two years before—people whispered he was at the bottom of Tampa Bay because of some drug deal.

Agnes and Daryl sat down at a corner booth and ordered

coffee. "I can't stay in this town," said Daryl, staring at the table.

"Of course you can. You were wonderful in *Buffalo*. They need you."

"I don't give a rat's ass if they need me. I can't face that group again."

There was a pause. Then Agnes said, "*I* need you." They were both holding on to their coffee cups like mendicants in the street.

"You need me least of all. You're the strong one."

In the silence that followed, Agnes looked up. When her eyes widened, Daryl turned and saw three young men seated on the turnstools with their backs to the counter, looking at once unfocused and malevolent. Their black vests and boots, their heavy grease-stained levis, far too hot for Florida, their tattoos: a biker's outfit has more clichés than a banker's. The tallest one had spurs on his boots; the other two wore chains for belts. Agnes recognized the tall one, but didn't know his name.

"Hello, Aggie," he said. "You still my sweetheart?"

The question was so bizarre that Agnes said nothing. The bikers slid off their seats and slouched toward the door in that threatening stroll they have mastered.

"So long, lover," the tall one said. "See you at The Grouper."

In a few minutes they heard the motorcycles cough and roar away; the bikes had been parked in the back, out of sight. The two sat silently for a long moment. "I do not care about brave or cowardly!" Agnes said suddenly. "No one knows what that means anyway. I want someone who has sense, good sense!" She spoke this defiantly, holding Daryl's eyes. "Who will live a long time!" she almost shouted.

A stout woman with peroxided hair was staring at them from the next table with such intensity that Daryl leaned over and handed her the ketchup. The woman shifted her stare from the couple to the bottle, sitting there as if hypnotized by the Heinz label.

"I'll tell you something about me," Daryl said. "You know that accident I told you about?" He hesitated. "Where I got these scars? Well, there wasn't any girl. Just some stupid kids. Horsing around. I made it all up so you'd be interested in me. But it's all lies. I wasn't even driving."

"No," she said. "Of course not."

"I'm a liar. I'm stupid."

Agnes smiled as naturally as if she had been smiling all her life. "I do not love you because you are smart. I love you because you are beautiful."

Their dispirited waitress had perfected the eye-on-the-floor and seemed to take forever to get to them, but at last they were outside on the dark tree-lined street heading toward Central Avenue.

"What's the sensible thing to do?" he asked after another long silence.

"That is what you must decide."

He had already decided, and was steering them back through the sad streets, sweetened a little by the rich smell of old flowering trees with the lovely names: jacaranda, bougainvillea, magnolia, mimosa. He knew he was right because she held his hand tighter as they neared The Grouper. The party was still going on, more or less, though the noise was subdued and sober. Robertson was sitting at the head of a long scarred table, apparently declaiming a speech from some play. They watched through the window for a minute.

"Some show," said Daryl.

"Yes," she agreed. "Some show."

"Well, let's get our tickets." He pushed the door open and they walked in.

II
From Abroad

A Decent
Life

Hannah Broch didn't like the way her husband dressed, drank, drove, walked, talked, cleared his throat, made love (too noisy) or water (likewise). In the morning he'd try to fold his pajamas, but they always looked like a lump. His belly was large and soft. He was one of those people who, given, say, a telephone number, could concentrate on it for a few seconds and almost immediately would not only have forgotten the number but whose it was and to whom he was talking. In the evening he'd waddle in smelling of beer and try to kiss her. She could have poked his eyes out. And now he had a mistress! She could have kicked in his teeth.

Hannah shook her head sometimes, wondering why she held on to the little bastard. The truth was, she was competitive. She would rather pull out her hair and set it on fire than lose at anything, whether it was cards or cribbage, chess or conversation. To get a divorce, then, would be to admit a great defeat, and she was not about to do it. Therefore, when she discovered her husband was having an affair, she called the Authorities. She was uncertain what they would do, or even what they were supposed to do, but she knew they were there—they were everywhere—and they had ways of smoothing over all difficulties. People often resented the amount of paperwork generated by the Authorities, but everyone admitted they got the job done, and life was better.

She had first become suspicious when Stefan began whistling again. Before they were married he had been a great whistler; he had a real talent for it. He liked best the famous arias from operas like *Pagliacci* or *Carmen*—he would prance like Escamillo the bullfighter when he whistled the toreador tune—but he could also whistle from works like *Tosca*, long stretches that nobody else could remember. After a few years of marriage, however, they had stopped going to the opera, and soon after that he had stopped whistling.

"Hannah says we can't go, she has nothing to wear," Stefan would explain to their friends. "And she's perfectly right, she *has* nothing to wear." He'd spread his hands out. They were soft and pudgy, stained with purple ink from the stamp pad at the post office where he worked as a clerk all week. The pay was low, and by now there was little chance of advancement, but they had enough to eat and a comfortable apartment on Krolewska Street, nicer than most of their friends', and in a good section of the city, though all the sections nowadays were more or less alike. At any rate, people no longer moved from job to job, but stuck with the one they were assigned and hoped for the best.

There are two basic attitudes toward life: when confronted with the possibility of a new experience, you can either say *yes* or say *no*. Both answers are correct and will be equally regretted, experience being what it is. But the attitudes are incompatible and cause most of the difficulties between married couples. In the early years of their marriage Hannah and Stefan quarreled along those basic lines. Stefan would want to leave the city, or even the country, change jobs, collect butterflies, buy a car, have children; Hannah would point out the impossibility, the danger, of these ideas. They weren't ready, they couldn't afford it, their apartment was too small, they had no contacts. Because she was the stronger of the two, they had settled down and were reasonably secure. He had stopped whistling, but that was all right with her: she was tone-deaf and mainly held the impression of his fat cheeks puffing in and out, in and out.

Stefan, like many others, was neither a leader nor a follower: he was a loner. People tend to mistake loners for leaders—this was Hannah's mistake when she met him—but in truth, most of them make atrocious decisions for others: their abilities are limited to their own rhythms. So it was with Stefan, at any rate, who had had his chances that he didn't really want and had blown them completely, to the chagrin of his more ambitious wife. Once, replacing someone who was sick, Stefan directed a small branch post office for three months and caused so much confusion with the first-class mail that there was a military investigation.

In most ways, except for his corpulence, he was a nondescript man. He wore a modest beard and too-small wire glasses that he was always pushing up his nose with a one-fingered gesture that made him go cross-eyed. At parties women didn't notice him until late in the evening: he had a kind of staying power, the ability to look hopeful after midnight, that touched their hearts, particularly as the men of that district tended to drink themselves into oblivion. Someone gave him a cruelly affectionate nickname, the Social Butterball, an appellation that made him smile but turned a knife in his wife's heart. How undignified to be married to the Social Butterball!

Hannah hadn't paid close attention to his habits for many years, but when the whistling started she came alive again as her competitive juices began to flow. Stefan noticed her renewed attractiveness right away. She was a large, handsome woman with a deep voice and a mane of dark hair piled on top of her head. She had an ample bosom that was almost formidable, if such a word can be applied to those feminine softnesses. This was in marked contrast to Eva, who had almost no bosom at all. Eva, in fact, with her slender figure and short blonde hair looked like a young boy, and this combined with her wide gray eyes gave her such an air of vulnerability that Stefan's heart had reached out for her as soon as she entered the post office about six months before. She had had some complication in paying her telephone bill, and Stefan had made it seem even more complicated than it was, so she had to come see him several times and he had the opportunity to ask her to lunch. Thus the affair had begun.

Their city was not a happy one, to generalize wildly, but it had an erotic atmosphere, which was perhaps connected to its unhappiness. The weather was often cold, and the women wore tall boots and long skirts, and all one saw of their legs was the back of a knee or the top of a calf as they got on a bus or settled themselves on sofas. Stefan got a very Victorian *frisson* from such glimpses. The Victorians had many difficulties with sex, but at least they knew it was important. Yes, that was it: Stefan was a Victorian out of place in the New World.

Their affair was very tender. In her apartment, to which they would go during the long lunch break when her roommate was absent, she would stand shyly and passively with her arms at her side while he fumbled and trembled with her hooks and buttons. In bed he would say, "Do you like this? Do you like this?" and she would murmur, "Yes. Yes. I like everything about you. I like everything you do."

And she loved the opera. Sometimes they would just lie there while he whistled scores from *Traviata* or *Madame Butterfly*. She was his Carmen, he was her Don José. The fact that these stories ended with corpses littering the stage gave a certain poignancy to his whistling.

Hannah certified the existence of the affair in a very old-fashioned way: she found blonde hairs on his coat (he was *such* a pig!). Possessing a shrewdness that her husband lacked, she said nothing the first two times. Once could be an accident, twice could be a coincidence, but three times is a pattern, and it was then that she called the Authorities. The voice on the wire had been noncommittal, as always.

"With whom is your husband having an affair?"

"I don't know. A blonde."

"Where does he work?"

"At the main post office."

"Thank you."

And that was all, the voice hung up. It had been surprisingly easy, Hannah thought. She had expected a long interrogation, perhaps demands for proof. The voice had given the impression of competence, of knowledge in this area, of efficiency derived from long and woeful experience. It was hard to tell if the voice belonged to a man or a woman. Hannah hoped it was a woman; men really were brutes, after all. She sat back, narrowing her eyes when her husband came home whistling virtuoso riffs from *Figaro,* closing them entirely when he made that disgusting throat-clearing sound, and waited.

Three weeks later, on his desk at the post office, Stefan saw the familiar blue envelope with the eagle stamped on it. Now what? he thought with irritation. He was sure all his bills were paid. A new tax? Something he said at a party? No one liked to get the blue envelopes; they were always trouble, even if it were just some computer mix-up, which was often the case. He tore it open, hoping his co-workers hadn't seen it. But who put it there?

It was simply a notice that he had an appointment at 13:45 on Tuesday—that was today!—in Room 4230h at the Central Office. Nothing else. Just that and the eagle embossed over an indecipherable signature. Stefan's hands began to sweat, what bad luck! He was supposed to meet Eva at 2:00, but her room was in the other direction, and as she had no phone there was no way for him to get in touch with her. She would be worried, poor thing. In the new system most offices had a rotating lunch break, and they had arranged theirs to be from 1:30 to 3:00. What a lot of nonsense this was! Stefan muttered all morning, giving people the wrong change, banging their packages into the big bins. Just let somebody try to get smart with him! Bam! Into the bin went another package. At 1:25 a young woman in maternity clothes, with wispy hair and a drawn face, came to his window with four large packages. He studied the first package, frowning, for some time, weighed it, stamped it, tossed it in the bin, pulled his window, and put up his OUT TO LUNCH sign while the woman stood there with her mouth open. He hurried out the back door.

Stefan blinked for a minute in the harsh winter sunlight. Snow was still hard-packed over the streets and sidewalks, and on the corners clusters of little old women—where do they find these creatures?—poked at the large piles with snow shovels consisting of a piece of plywood on a broom-handle. Real shovels were in short supply. He turned right, toward the old square. The new buildings, like the post of-fice where he worked, were all quite modern, big beehives of interchangeable cubicles. But the buildings in the old sec-tion, they were something else. There were still mysteries there, and shadows, beautiful carvings, spires and minarets, hidden staircases, stained-glass windows, all in miraculous and irrational profusion. There were constant rumors that they would all be torn down because they were inefficient to run, but Stefan hoped this was not true. The younger people didn't seem to care, but there were enough older ones left who could make things hot, even for the Authorities, if such a thing were done.

The Authorities' Central Offices were in the largest of the old baroque palaces untouched by the war. Usually when Stefan walked through the square in the Old City he would stop, twirling his umbrella, and admire the ancient clock on the Town Hall with its figures of Death, Greed, Lust, and

Time that turned mechanically on the hour while the heavy chimes rolled over the tiled rooftops. But today he was preoccupied and hurried onto the dark cobblestones of Celetna Street, turned the corner by the beerhall of the Two Cats, and arrived in front of the palace six minutes early. Wide stone steps led up to its many doors, but as usual in this city only one of the doors would be open, and there was always a crowd of pale men and women bumping into one another as they entered and left the building. "Excuse me, excuse me," he said, "excuse me," as he made his way into the cavernous hall where people seemed to scamper back and forth like the poor souls in Limbo, as if someone were tipping the floor so they would scurry first one way, then another. Plunged into the darkness of the hall after the bright light of outdoors, Stefan felt unbalanced, and he put a hand on a marble column to steady himself. Soon, between gaps in the ebbing and flowing crowd, he could make out in the gloom a single unmanned desk marked INFORMATION.

When he reached the desk, there was no one to help him, but behind it was a small sign with numbers and arrows; 4000–4499 had an arrow pointing to the left, so he struck off in that direction. The surgings of the crowd made more sense to him as he followed the arrows around corners, across hallways, down and up stairs, seemingly circling back on his steps as if in a mad hotel designed for minotaurs. At last he came to a dead end with an open elevator; he was surprised to find himself suddenly alone. Stefan stepped into the elevator and pushed 4, looking at his watch. But he was only three minutes late—he could hardly believe it, it seemed he had been walking for ages—as he scurried down a long, impersonal corridor where all the doors were the same except for the numbers and entered Room 4320h feeling absolutely and irrevocably guilty.

Stefan had always felt guilty when he was near the Palace, he didn't know why. He had been in their branch offices many times—visas, work permits, travel passes when he visited his sister in Katow—and he felt guilty in those places, too. Lord knows he had often said uncharitable things about the Authorities and had thought even worse. But he had never done anything even remotely subversive, outside of the little cheating on his sugar stamps that everybody did. Still, he felt guilty. He even felt guilty about feeling guilty. It seemed to be part of his temperament. If he didn't buy anything in a grocery store, for example, he would all but disrobe on the way out to prove he had stolen nothing. Since the beginning of his affair with Eva, despite surges of enormous happiness, he felt he was swimming in Guilt Soup, a thick broth of his own concoction. Therefore, facing the stern-visaged indeterminate-aged woman who stared at him from behind a large, well-ordered desk, he was tempted to cry out, "I confess!!" instead of the weak "Good afternoon" he finally managed.

She asked his name. He told her. His address, age, occupation. She was a short lean woman with spectacles, almost a caricature of what a strict Latin teacher is supposed to look like. It was not a face that fitted easily into a smile.

"You are overweight?" she asked. "You eat too much?"

He didn't answer. He wasn't sure he heard right. For one thing, the answer was obvious. For another, what was this, a medical examination? He looked around the room. For the first time he saw the soldier standing motionless by an inner door.

She repeated the question. Her voice was like an iron bell.

"Yes." His knees began to shake. There seemed to be no place to sit down. It was as if he knew what the next question would be, and he shuffled his feet in an attempt to postpone it.

"You are having an affair with Eva Levandoska, yes?"

"No," he said, and she looked up at him so suddenly, so sharply, that he said, "Yes. Yes," he said, looking not at her but at the soldier, who was just a boy, though tall and stock-ily built. "Do I have to answer these questions?"

The matron's face turned black, and she shouted, "How can you justify such piggish, antisocial behavior?" She stared at him with such violence that he almost fell down.

Stefan swallowed, or tried to. He had never thought his behavior was justifiable. But he raised his chin and said in a quavering voice, "I think when two people come together in love, it is a kind of miracle."

She stared at him. "Perhaps. But it is an inevitable mira-cle." She said the word sneeringly. "Repetitious. Childish. And basically harmful to society."

Stefan regretted he had said "miracle." He didn't want to get into a religious argument with the Authorities. Being half-Jewish put him in a difficult spot. His Jewish friends, Peter and Bo—two of the few Jews left in the city—were always afraid. But of what? They no longer seemed to know. In the old days Stefan's father had taught him not to talk about religion. "Religion is all right," he'd say, lopping the head off a chicken. "It just doesn't apply to every case. That's why we have the Authorities."

But the woman dropped the subject and went on with her questions, her voice once again controlled and low. She con-tinued in this way for some time, asking the most intimate questions, as if this were a civil service test. Positions? Per-versities? Did he sweat a lot? Stefan, answering, head down, in barely audible monosyllables, was sweating profusely, his shirt soaked and sticking to his skin. Was the soldier listen-ing? He made no sign.

"You are noisy?"

"Pardon me?"

"When you copulate, you are very noisy, yes?"

Stefan looked around wildly. Hannah! They had talked to Hannah. She knew. She had turned him in! The matron had been staring at some papers, but now she looked up again.

She placed a photograph of Eva before him. "You admit everything, yes?"

Stefan didn't hesitate; his heart was beating so hard he could scarcely hear anything. "Yes. Yes, I do." He couldn't look at her. Instead he found himself staring at a small printed placard on the left side of her desk, by a calendar, that said PASSION AND THE DECENT LIFE ARE INCOMPATIBLE.

"Good," she said, standing up and pushing a document at him. "We understand each other, I hope. Please sign here. And here." Somehow she looked smaller when she stood up. Her dress was black or dark blue and hung on her shapelessly. She looked at her watch. "You still have half an hour," she said in a businesslike tone. "That should be enough time. Please take off your clothes."

"Pardon me?"

"Take off your clothes," she repeated sternly but not unkindly, as if to someone retarded. "Hang them by the door and go in." The door was by the soldier, an immovable statue. The matron sat down, busy at her desk. Stefan stood behind her, on the right, in front of the uniformed boy who now seemed to Stefan to have the bland face of a killer, a mass murderer. Stefan had always hated uniforms, even policemen and Boy Scouts, and he was terrified as he disrobed in front of this robot. Oh, God, God, God, he thought, they're going to kill me, they're going to gas me and take the gold fillings out of my teeth. And my new shoes.

But he was not a fighter. Not knowing what else to do, he hung his clothes on the hooks by the inner door, dropping them several times, and, feeling ridiculous and defenseless standing naked with his round and hairy belly shaking between the matron and the soldier, he turned and plunged through the door, which the soldier immediately closed behind him.

It was a small room, bare except for a large clock hanging on the green wall, and a medium-sized cot. Even in his fright he felt the lowered temperature, and he shivered. Just as he noticed a door opposite from where he had entered, it opened, and Stefan backed into a corner with a strangled cry. A figure came toward him, coming into focus as the door closed behind it.

It was Eva. She looked at him with the startled eyes of an animal, tried to cover herself, then ran to him. Both of them began to cry as they embraced, rocking back and forth in the corner of this barren room where the clock loudly ticked to 14:08. They kissed. They sat down on the cot. He pulled a blanket over them; they were both shaking from cold and fright.

"They've been watching us," Eva said. "They know everything."

"I know. But what do they want with us? What are they going to do?" Suddenly from behind the wall by their cot came a series of gasps and moans. After their initial fright, it soon became clear to them that a couple was making love in the adjoining room.

For a while Eva and Stefan were silent and embarrassed. They felt their nakedness as if for the first time. Stefan awkwardly embraced her.

"Stefan, I can't."

Stefan looked down. "I *obviously* can't." But this made them laugh, and they huddled together under the covers. The sounds from the next room started up again. They lay with their arms around each other, and as the clock ticked to 14:22 he was surprised to find himself excited. They didn't speak; they seemed to be in a situation in which nothing they could say would make any sense.

They were scarcely finished when the door opened and the matron looked in. Did she nod approvingly? "Yes," she said, "time's up." Stefan almost ran to the open door, not even looking back at Eva, sitting up on the cot with the covers clutched to her chin. He dressed before the unblinking soldier in a fury of shame and fear, and hardly heard the woman as she announced, "Your next appointment is at 14:00 a week from tomorrow. We will send you a reminder." Stefan went blindly out the door, through the corridor, down the elevator, following the arrows in reverse order until he reached the front door. It was impossible, but the sun was still shining, though thinner now, and the old clock on the Town Hall was just striking three. Death was ringing its bell, Time waved its sickle. Greed and Lust made ambiguous movements with their hands. Stefan stared up at them, transfixed in complicated thought.

He was late for work already, but he was too shaky to go back to the post office anyway. He could call in sick. He looked around for Eva in the crowd, but she was nowhere to be seen. He decided to head for home.

On the long walk back to Krolewska Street through the already darkening city, Stefan began to cry. He cried for perhaps a half a mile, passersby stepping aside as he approached. But by the time he neared his apartment he was feeling better. The tears stopped. For the first time in months, he realized, he did not feel guilty. He was free! He had an image of his heart bobbing to the surface from a dark and densely pressured depth. The relief was so great that he was surprised by a rush of affection for his wife. She had known what to do after all. And what were Authorities for if not to lighten the burdens of their citizens? He took a deep, deep breath. Twirling his umbrella, Stefan waddled up the steps and into his flat. Hannah sat in the big chair, chin held high, drumming her fingers on the armrest. He went up to her, put his hand on her shoulders, began to whistle, stopped, and cleared his throat.

The
Twisted
River

"What's black and white and runs away when you call it?" the American asked.

Domanski was squinting at the menu, holding it up to the candle. "I give up."

"A Polish waiter!" The American barked three or four times at his own joke, and Domanski tried to smile. He had heard them all and hated them with a fierce passion. As he smiled he reached out in his imagination and broke the American's nose by twisting it sharply to the right.

The American's name was Dan Bradley; he was tall and well built, with wavy hair turned prematurely gray. He was handsome in a weak and romantic way, almost pretty, despite his long breakable nose. Bradley had deep-set dark eyes with long lashes and a high intellectual forehead, which was, like much of his appearance, totally misleading. He was a teacher of applied linguistics at a small Southern college and, despite his Ph.D., had scarcely read a real book in his life. This year he was teaching on a Fulbright at a Polish university, leaving his wife and children at home, and had just astounded Domanski not simply by his ignorance but by his ignorance of his ignorance. In their first ten minutes of conversation Domanski had discovered that Bradley had never even heard of either Edward Gierek or Joseph Conrad. How was that possible? Jesus Christ, what are the Americans trying to do, he thought, sabotage the whole program? Americans were chauvinistic and contemptuous of other cultures, but Bradley seemed to be an extreme case. What on earth could they talk about?

"How is your apartment?" Domanski was the University man in charge of making the way smooth for the American professors.

"It stinks, babes, but that's not what I want to talk to you about. It's about Bubin." Bradley leaned across the table, his hair close to the candle flame, and paused dramatically. "Did you know he was queer?"

Domanski still pretended to study the menu. Polish restaurants tended to be dark, romantically (and economically) candlelit, with a menu typed on a fourth carbon, so you could spend hours trying to make it out. They seldom had what was on the menu anyway, and it was best to rely on the judgment of the waiter. Finally Domanski said, "Bubin is one of our best teachers."

"I bet," said Bradley, "but he's queer as a green kielbasa."

Domanski ordered a double vodka. In his three years of dealing with American professors he had come to like them as a group: they were generally hardworking, open, generous, popular with students. They got drunk often and those with shaky marriages tended to run off with the pretty Polish coeds, and this made them seem more human to Domanski, who took the long view on moral questions. But Bradley was something else—he didn't even drink, and sipped a glass of mineral water throughout the dinner.

"Well," Domanski said after a while, "I don't know anything about it. But why tell me, it's none of my business." *Or yours*, he wanted to add.

"Because he made a pass at me," said Bradley, "and I want you to fire the bastard."

Domanski coughed into his vodka and the candle flame whirled and flickered, giving Bradley's lean face a Satanic glow. "I can't do that, even if I wanted to. He outranks me. Why don't you just forget about it and stay away from him? We're not kids, after all. Where's the harm?"

"Listen, Tadeusz," said Bradley, "you can do it. Let's be frank. I know you're a member of the Party and Bubin isn't. You have pull, and they'll be glad to get rid of him." He stood up and threw a 500-zloty note on the table. "If you won't do it, nice and quietly, I'll do it myself, very *un*-quietly, and you'll be a very sorry ex-professor." He held Domanski's eyes with his own for a long moment and then strode out of the restaurant.

For a long time Domanski sat by himself, sipping his vodka. In the shadowy room, with its wide-beamed ceiling and dark wooden furniture, the whisperings of the other diners floated like scented smoke. It smelled like—like secrets, Domanski thought. The man at the next table leaned forward, his hand on the thigh of the young woman across from him. Everyone had secrets, and why not? That was why we wore clothes and had polite conversations. Secrets were the moral equivalent of private property; in this respect, Domanski was a thoroughgoing capitalist. Informers were universally hated because they broke the unwritten moral law of the right to secrets.

And he was an informer himself: he was trapped. The odd English phrase came to him: hoist with his own petard.

Domanski went outside and stood breathing in the cold night air. The snow muffled the sounds of the city and he stared at the darkened windows of the huge apartment buildings. Each building was an anthology of secrets, most of them boring: he didn't want to know them. When the tram banged by, he got on and went home; his wife was asleep and he lay down gently beside her. She stirred as he settled in, and muttered in her sleep, "Don't do that, you shouldn't do that." Domanski watched her for a while, her full white breasts rising and falling in the darkness. After nine years she was as appealing to him as when she was his student, but what did he really know about her, what were her secrets?

Tadeusz Domanski—Tadek to his friends—was a small, nervous man with light-colored hair and an almost invisible mustache. "It's an intimate mustache," he liked to say, his pale quick eyes squinting when he smiled. He was well organized, absolutely fluent in English, having spent two postgraduate years at Yale, and had published a book on the American projectivist poets. He didn't understand them very well, but, then, who did? He took the position that they were the last of the Romantics, and since there was no one qualified to criticize his judgment he was made an assistant professor on the basis of that book.

Bradley scared him. Domanski was ambitious, and to get ahead in Poland you needed to belong to the Party, or at least get along with it. He was not actually a member—Bradley was wrong there—but in the past, when he had been asked, he had helped them out by reporting on various activities within the University, all very innocuous and harmless. His conscience was fairly clear. That was the catch: just fairly clear. He kept track of the Americans for the Party, what they were doing, where they were going. And of his colleagues: who wanted to go abroad, and why. His recommendation was important, and he used it, as far as possible, to help his department and his friends. But how had Bradley found out about his connection, or was he just bluffing? And what could possibly be done about Bubin?

Tomasz Bubin was one of his best friends, and Domanski had known for a long time that he was homosexual. He knew he should have reported this—in these matters the Party was more prudish and vindictive than the Church— but up to now it had been an easy thing to avoid. Quite simply, Bubin was the most brilliant person in the department, the best teacher, and perhaps the best literary critic in the country; and this had seemed all that was necessary to say about him. Everyone took for granted that Bubin would become chairman next year, upon the retirement of old Professor Nowak, an event eagerly anticipated by the entire staff. A few, like Domanski, knew that Bubin was homosexual, and many others guessed—a successful unmarried man of forty—and in a way they were proud of it. See, Poland is liberal, flexible, modern: it was like having their own Whitman or Auden or Ginsberg, and they were secretly pleased. But now, suddenly, everything seemed complicated. In a public discussion old rumors that Bubin's mother had been Jewish were likely to resurface. These days Jewishness was at least as dangerous as homosexuality, and Domanski had not tried to verify the rumors. So it was not just Bubin's job that hung in the balance but his own, depending on how he handled the situation.

The next day he made an appointment to see Bubin at three o'clock, after Bubin's classes. Domanski was so nervous that he could hardly eat lunch and became almost tipsy from the beer he drank. He bumped into people on the stairway, tore his sleeve on a door handle, and in general behaved in a way that made people stare at him, making him more jumpy than ever. In class he confused Berryman with Lowell, got angry when a student corrected him, and dismissed the whole class early. They scuttled out, clutching their books and whispering among themselves. In the hallway he heard Bradley's barking laugh and tried to avoid him, but the American caught up to him and put his long fingers on Domanski's shoulders.

"Have you done anything yet?"

"No, of course not. What can I do?"

Bradley smiled. Americans had hateful white teeth. "If you don't, I will, babes." Why did he call everyone "babes"? "I'll be in touch." Domanski stared at Bradley's nose and then abruptly turned and went upstairs to his own office.

At three o'clock he knocked on Bubin's door and entered. Bubin was shuffling through some papers on the desk he shared with Dr. Kaminska, who only came in on Tuesdays and Thursdays. None of the offices had books in them, just desks, a blackboard, some chairs, and a cabinet where they kept toilet paper, soap, and chalk. For the first time Domanski saw how much like a cell, or interrogation room, the offices were. That, he thought, must be how the students saw them.

"Hello, Tadek." Bubin leaned back, stretching his arms. "What's up?"

Domanski's head was spinning; the walls seemed to be breathing in and out, and his stomach had that elevator feeling. "Well, Tomek, something's come up. It's about Professor Bradley . . ." What was he going to say?

"That asshole! Linguists are always weird, but this one is totally incompetent." Bubin shook his head. He had electric blue eyes, a full beard, and the charisma that certain ugly and highly energetic people possessed. When he entered a room you felt his presence immediately. "Don't worry about Bradley," he said. "That's the last time we're going to hire an applied linguist. He teaches the students as if they were in kindergarten, and they laugh at him behind his back."

"I've heard that," said Domanski, stalling for time. "But how did he get a Fulbright? He must know something."

"How did he get a Ph.D.? That's the big question. Well, he's a manipulator. He's got the American Embassy snowed, he brings flowers to the secretaries, he complains, he works one person against another, he tries to charm the ladies, he pressures everyone to write letters of recommendation, he takes people out to dinner . . ."

"Yes, he took *me* out last night . . ." Domanski began.

"He's hard to resist, he makes it very personal," Bubin continued. "That's how he got his Ph.D. If you fail me I'll jump out the window!" Bubin laughed, waving his arms. "He wants to teach here a second year, he's out of a job in the

States, he needs the money, his poor starving children! He can be very persuasive, but I've dug in and said no. We have our students to think about. And ourselves," he added. "You know, I've been to his apartment and there's not a single book or magazine in it, outside of a few linguistic textbooks. No novels, no poetry, nothing. It's incredible! Nowak of course can't handle him—he's too softhearted—so he's left it up to me."

"Tomek, listen to me. He's going to accuse you of being homosexual." Domanski had been standing and now sat down heavily and stared at the floor. In the silence that followed, Bubin lit a cigarette. There were no ashtrays, and he dropped the match into an empty wine bottle on the desk.

After a while Bubin said, "Tell me exactly what he said." His voice, after its previous exuberance, was soft and low. Domanski could hardly hear him.

"He said you made a pass at him. He wants me to get you fired or he'll denounce you himself."

Bubin blew out a great cloud of smoke. His hands were trembling. He spoke slowly. "What did *you* say?"

"I said I couldn't do it. I said I didn't know anything about it."

"Thank you, Tadek. But of course you do know. It's no secret; at least, not much of one." Bubin pulled on his beard. "That bastard." He put his cigarette into the bottle and lit another. "It's tough enough to be a fag anywhere, I suppose, but here . . ." Bubin made a slashing motion across his throat. "And the thing is, he's lying through those big white teeth. Doesn't he remind you of a horse, Tadek? The idea of making a pass at him makes my stomach turn."

"But, then, what proof does he have? We can just ignore him."

"He doesn't need proof. Even *that* wouldn't be proof. No, Bradley has the mind of a weasel: he finds out what he needs to find out by sniffing in all the corners. He lives on the telephone, that's his idea of homework." Bubin let himself smile a little. "He probably knows that Klapocz is an alcoholic and that Pokop sleeps with his students. And, Tadek, he guesses, as most of us have, that you're connected with the Party. The Americans probably told him—they have their own network. That's why he went to you." Bubin stood up and began pacing around the office, a cigarette in one hand and the wine bottle in the other. "There are small secrets everywhere," he said, echoing Domanski's thoughts of the previous evening. "Secrets nobody cares about, as long as the work is getting done and there's not a big flap about it. They give a human texture to our little community, but at the same time they make it fragile and vulnerable, and people like Bradley can exploit it."

Domanski chewed at a fingernail. "Tomasz, why don't we just rehire him for another year? That's probably all he wants, and then he'll be gone. Fulbrighters can only stay for two years."

Bubin paused. "Not always," he said, "some stay longer. But yes, there are three possibilities. We could take him back for next year. But can we trust him? And think how distasteful that would be. Or I could resign and transfer to the provinces." He made a face. "Or we could murder him, chop his body up into little pieces and dump him into the Vistula. That's the one I favor, though it does pose certain difficulties." He laughed. "These days they're restricting dumping garbage into the river!

"All right, my good friend," he continued, "let me think about it and I'll call you sometime tomorrow."

"Are you all right?" Domanski's wife asked when they were in bed that night. "Your hands are like ice."

"Yes, I just feel stretched tight, I don't know why. I'm all right." But he couldn't sleep. His wife's round white arm lay across his stomach, and when she began to snore softly he slid from beneath it and stood for a long time naked at the window. Across the street the government building with its tall iron gate and innumerable dark windows blocked out the moon. It was not a sympathetic building: who could he talk to there? Poland is the only country with a prejudice against its own citizens, someone had said at a party, and everyone laughed. But where could he turn? If Bubin goes, I go, he thought suddenly, surprising himself. I'll go to the provinces, too; when the Party calls, I won't answer. All his life he had worked for the secure position he now held, and the thought of throwing it over made him dizzy. He sat down in the ancient armchair that he loved so much and chewed his fingernails until they bled.

The following morning he stayed home, waiting for Bubin's telephone call, which never came. From outside, the chanting cry of the rag lady with her straw basket floated through his window like a mournful ghost. He sat in his armchair, drinking tea, turning the situation this way and that until he came to a resolution.

Bradley seemed like a hard man to talk to, but who knows? Maybe he was just insecure, afraid for his future, like everyone else. The main problem was Bradley's almost total ignorance of literature: he had no idea of Bubin's importance, his brilliance, vulnerability, sensitivity. Bubin's book on the American novel was the best that anyone had ever done. Domanski's idea was to present Bubin as some sort of national treasure; perhaps even Bradley would understand. Maybe he could be talked into a post at another university. There seemed to be, in the light of a new day, various possibilities that they hadn't considered, and by lunch time Domanski felt a little better.

At mid-afternoon he went to the University. The normality of the scene was reassuring: the students hurrying in clusters under the dark branches of the chestnut trees, the dignified old buildings with their Corinthian columns, the cozy corner where the Institute of English was tucked away from the main traffic of the campus. Neither Bubin nor Bradley was in his office. Domanski's office was a garret on the fourth floor, at the top of a narrow staircase. He sat down at his barren desk and called for his mail, which was brought up in a few minutes by a student assistant. Among the usual announcements and notices was a large manilla envelope. Domanski pulled out a heavy manuscript, a thick collection of poems. On the title page was typed *The Twisted River, by B.T.* The *B.T.* was crossed out and beneath it, handwritten in bold letters, was *Tomasz Bubin.*

Domanski's heart lurched and he had to steady himself on his desk. The radical poems of B.T.—fierce, powerful, patriotic, anti-Russian—had been appearing in underground magazines for several years and the identity of the poet had been the center of much controversy. Many people tended to think the poems were the work of some dissident safely out of the country, like Milosc or Krynicki, but that never made sense to Domanski—they would use their own names, and besides, it was a new voice, singular, unmistakably original. He had been asked by the Party about these poems, but he had known nothing. And all along it had been Bubin, working in the room right below him!

With shaking hands he pulled out a letter written on yellow paper and tucked into the manuscript. He recognized Bubin's precise handwriting.

My dear Tadek, the letter began, *So, you see, there are secrets inside of secrets. I am very tired, but I will try not to be sentimental. This manuscript cannot be mailed, of course, and I am trusting you because I know you are trustworthy, despite your "connections." Please deliver this manuscript yourself, or through one of your American friends, to the Institut Litteraire in Paris. Give it to Mr. Gleboski, who will see that it is published and distributed. I am counting on you to do this last thing for me.*

I have made too many mistakes, many that you don't know about, and I regret them all. I have regretted them for a long time. One of the worst mistakes was with Bradley: he told you the truth about me, and I lied. I feel an enormous disgust for myself when I think about it, but it is too late now. It is just as well. I will not leave Poland, which I have always loved beyond words. I will not go anywhere. I would like to be buried at Powazkowski, near the other writers, but that is not important.

I have no faith in myself, but I have faith in the voice that has spoken through me, for Poland, our tragic and beloved country, and for all of us who have wanted a more meaningful and free existence. That is why the manuscript is so important. Tadek, I am depending on you. I know I can. Peace. Tomasz.

For several minutes Domanski stared at the letter as if hypnotized. He had trouble focusing his eyes. He had trouble breathing. Then he grabbed the phone and dialed Bubin's number, misdialing twice with his fumbling fingers, until finally he got it to ring. There was no answer.

He carefully placed the manuscript and letter in his desk drawer and locked it. Pulling on his coat, he rushed out of the room and down the stairs. But on the landing outside of the English office he met Bradley, who turned to him with his wide white smile and reached out as if to detain him. Domanski knew that Bradley could tear him apart so he had to be quick. With all his might he hit Bradley flush on the nose and felt the bone splinter as they both fell down on the floor, rolling over and over like demented lovers.

Sealink

Emily had never hit a sheep before. Two years ago she had run over a dog right after Howard said, "This is a thirty-five-mile-an-hour zone, you know." It took a long time for her to forgive him for that, and then he had left anyway.

Only a thin sliver of blood slid from the sheep's nose, but it was dead all right. She wondered what the penalty was for killing a sheep in Normandy. *Sheep Assassin's Head Shaved. Bury Her in Mint Jelly, Advises Mayor.* Emily wondered if her French was up to the task of explanation. I was just inching along, officer, when this bloody sheep charged me.

There had been no way to avoid the accident. She always drove a *little* above the speed limit and as she took her rented Ford over the hill the sheep popped up in front and a big Mercedes crowded her from the other side. She could easily have been killed, but the Mercedes never even slowed down. For once she must have been wearing her seat belt (first the good news, she thought . . .), and all she suffered was a pretty good bump on the head, but nothing broken. The car, however, wouldn't go: the left front headlight and fender were smashed, and it looked like the wheel was bent. Something was jammed, at any rate.

Emily had rented the car in London and had taken the Sealink ferry from Weymouth to Cherbourg. FATHER DIED YESTERDAY STOP, the telegram from her brother had said, CAN YOU COME HOME FUNERAL TUESDAY. Her brother's telegrams never ran over ten words, and she could imagine him thinking where to put the STOP: FATHER DIED YESTERDAY

CAN YOU COME HOME STOP . . . She would have preferred
STOP FATHER DIED YESTERDAY CAN YOU COME HOME, but that
was the difference between the two of them. Her brother was
probably right.

She should have answered him: gestures were important,
even if they were misunderstood. She should have said,
NEVER STOP NEVER STOP NEVER STOP NEVER STOP NEVER STOP.
Her father would have liked that. He was a crusty and acid-
tongued professor with whom she had argued bitterly; she
had no intention of flying all the way to Boston to see his
dead body. He would have ridiculed the idea. God knows she
had reached out her hand to him over and over, only to have
the miserable old bastard turn his back. Still, something felt
called for and, compelled by a dark fluttering within her
breast, a vague flashing of knives, an unfocused fear that ran
like a spider along her nerves and veins, she had rented the
car and left the city. It took several hours for her to realize
she was headed for Mont St. Michel, and even now she was
not sure why.

Her father had taken them there years ago, when they
were children, and she had been bored. All Emily wanted to
do was race up and down the steep steps while her mother
and brother dutifully listened to his discourses on medieval
methods of building; Roman, Gothic, Baroque styles of architecture; and monastical rules. She of course was soon lost
in the crowded and twisting lanes, and at their tearful re-
union had been forced to endure lectures by both parents
and told-you-so smirks from her brother.

But as she drove out of London—was that just yesterday?—the stark and jagged image of the ancient abbey gradually formed in her mind, just as it had soared from the fog-
bound marshland outside of Pontorson, and she was drawn
like a tired swimmer by the tide: she remembered it much
more clearly than she would have thought. The monastery
was about a hundred kilometers south of Cherbourg and she

had reached—she imagined—about halfway down the coast when she hit the sheep. She really didn't know where she was. The last sign had said Coustances, but whether Coustances was ahead or behind she had no idea. She supposed the sea was on her right, but all she could see were rolling green hills, clusters of pear trees, a few sheep munching grass near the road, and a bevy of fat white geese inside a small fenced-in area in the middle of nowhere.

Where was everybody? Perhaps everyone in France slept in on Mondays, after the excesses of the weekend. Emily didn't want to walk away from the car, but she couldn't stay here forever. A lowslung Citroen, like a black cockroach, went by fast and honked without stopping.

There was something odd about the pear trees; they seemed closer than they had at first, but not clearer. The fruit was varicolored, splashes of red, yellow, and green more like a pointillist painting than actual pears. She could smell them, though, sweet and heavy to the senses, and as the shadows approached the car she could feel the air turn perceptibly cooler. She remembered suddenly a bowl of fruit she had shared with Howard, how long ago was that? They had been sitting along the rocky shore outside of Penzance, a little village called Mousehole, eating peaches and pears with Cornish clotted cream and some bottles of pale ale; a cool breeze blew in from the dark water. She had shivered and Howard held her in his arms, smiling but saying nothing. Was it possible to be happier than they were at that moment? Happiness was different from what she had believed, and quieter. The thought occurred to her that if you loved someone with all of your heart, even for a fraction of a second, then you would go to heaven. She looked at the dead sheep and said, "I think I'm going bonkers."

She had to do something: she couldn't just sit here twiddling like a Greek philosopher. Her father had been a man of action. By now he would have assembled the local police, a garage mechanic, and two insurance adjusters for appraisals and estimates of damage. As she thought this, however, a heavy lethargy took hold of her, not at all unpleasant. She had always preferred to stay still and let the world come around to her. She had observed her father's restlessness— even in the theater he seemed eager to get it over with, and on his many trips he was always rushing to get home: experience was just something to discuss, to swallow as abruptly as possible. Emily came to believe that what he really wanted was to die, wanted life itself to be over so that he could rest at last and talk it over with God. For this contrary reason she had moved slowly through her days, like a mermaid floating in a translucent sea where all was calm, shadowy, and ambiguous.

Emily liked ambiguity. She enjoyed being semi-lost, heading down a strange coast to Mont St. Michel, which she semi-remembered. An ambiguous world is a free world, rich with suggestion, each clear decision being a limiting factor: if you turn left, all the magical possibilities on the right are eliminated; to choose one thing is to cut out another.

As if to vindicate her lassitude, over the next rise in the road a dark object emerged that clarified, as it drew nearer, into a horsedrawn wagon with perhaps a dozen men on it, six on each side. They were singing a song that didn't sound French; perhaps it was Latin, and indeed they had a generally monk-like appearance, wearing rough brown capes and simple sandals. The horses were blinkered so they wouldn't shy from the high-speed cars, and their ribs showed, making a sharp contrast with the fat sheep and geese in the French countryside. The wagon slowly pulled even with Emily's Ford and shuddered to a stop with all the creaking of an ancient ship settling in its dock.

"*Pardonnez-moi,*" Emily said. "*Pouvez-vous m'aider?* Do you speak English?"

The nearest monk detached himself, grunting as he
dropped off the wagon, and peered into her back seat without
answering. "Nuffink to be done 'ere, is it?" he said, to no one
in particular. He had puffy androgynous lips that he
moistened every few seconds with his little pink tongue.
"You better come wiv me, darlin.'" His accent was very
Cockney, not unlike the barkeep at the King's Crown that
Howard had been so jealous of. " 'Ave anuvver pint, darlin',"
the barkeep would say, "you're the bes' fink wot ever comes
in 'ere." Once, on the back of a beer coaster in their usual
booth, someone had written:

Emmy woz ear wiv Bernard
She woz ear
Yes she woz
Woz she ear
Cors she woz
Emmy woz ear wiv Bernard

She hadn't known what to make of that. Was the barkeep
named Bernard? She was afraid to ask. Was it a poem? Was it
a joke? Emily thought if they kept going to the King's Crown
the mystery would eventually be solved, but Howard felt it
was too weird, and possibly dangerous—he didn't like her
name coupled with strange men—so they stopped going.
Maybe that was why they broke up: like yoked satellites in
orbit around a fixed star, they had been held together by the
sociability of the King's Crown. At home they argued over
what television programs to watch and how much Howard
drank.

"Come wiv me, darlin'," the man repeated, holding out
his hand, soft and pink as his tongue. With mixed feelings of
relief and apprehension Emily went with him to the wagon.
Her legs seemed strange and far away, but she felt warm,
sitting among all these men, the good bitter odor of hay and
sweat washing over her. The horses lurched forward in their

creaky traces once again, and they moved dreamily away from the damaged Ford. Almost immediately she relaxed— she was in someone else's hands, thank God—and the jostling of the wagon made her sleepy. The singing now was quieter and more sporadic; a pewter tankard was being passed around. *"Quelquechose à boire?"* the man next to her asked. He had a warty, not unkind face, and a huge belly trembling with a life of its own.

"Merci."

The mug was so heavy she had to use both hands, and at the same time she noticed that her dress had ridden up her thighs and the man was staring at her legs, which even to her seemed strikingly white and provocative. The drink was fruity, a fermented cider, sweet and thick; she took a small sip and passed it on to the pink-tongued man on her right, then pulled her dress down over her knees, though it was difficult to keep it there with the jouncing of the wagon along the country road. Despite her problems and discomfort she felt almost coquettish, twitching her skirt down among these monastic males who were probably seldom in such proximity to a female.

"I'm so sorry to trouble you," she said. "I just need to get to the nearest garage." What was the French word for "garage"? The word for gas was *"l'essence,"* she knew that, so she could always say, "la place óu vous achetez l'essence."

But the warty man said, *"De rien,"* and smiled back at her as if he understood. Of course monks were scholars, everyone knew that, they practically kept civilization alive during the Middle Ages. Emily had the sudden thought that she was becoming part of history, like the artists in the museum where she worked as an assistant cataloger. Her father had wanted her to be an artist, and was disappointed when she had given it up. "Now we're both catalogers," he had said when she told him she had joined the museum's staff. "We'll spend our time writing footnotes that later catalogers will prove obtuse." But he at least was pretty well known, having edited a number of textbooks and critical collections concerning metaphysical poetry and having taught courses in Donne, Crashaw, Vaughan, Herbert—poets she had scarcely glanced at. Her father had liked poetry that was difficult; she liked simple poems: "Songs of Innocence," the Cavaliers.

> Stone walls do not a prison make
> Nor iron bars a cage . . .

You could remember lines like that, how did that start?

> When Death with unconfinéd wings
> Hovers within my gates . . .

That sounded wrong, but Emily couldn't concentrate as the wagon jounced along the narrow road. They seemed almost to be staying in one place, like a French mime, with lots of knee action but no progress. Still, she had noticed a sign, VILLEDIEU-LES-POÊLES, so they *must* be getting somewhere. Maybe the landscape was approaching them, like Birnam Woods to Dunsinane. Although no gas station was in view, they were entering a small town between two rows of attached houses. It was broad daylight but lights were on behind most of the lace-curtained windows. Where there's electricity there's bound to be gas stations, Emily thought. And dead fish and squashed turtles—the works. The houses were surrounded by small plots of ragged sunflowers and neat woodpiles; the town had a gray worn look, comfortable, livable, if not exactly prosperous: France is doing all right, she thought. Around the front doors clustered fat round thick clumps of hydrangeas—pale blue, off-white, dusty rose—their ripe elegance setting off the old brick and plaster construction of the walls.

"*Ici, madame,*" said the heavy monk on her left. They had stopped at the last door of the first group of homes. The sunflowers in the field beyond nodded like tired women with broken teeth; a dark Romanesque church loomed from the other side of the field, and beyond that more houses stretched out as far as Emily could see.

"*Ma voiture,*" she began, "*est brisée . . .*"

"Nuffink for it, luv," said the first monk, his soft hands surprising her. She couldn't believe how strong he was as he lifted her down from the wagon. "Time to rest; everyone's buggered."

"I'm not tired," Emily protested, "*pas fatiguée,*" but even as she said it she could feel her head nodding, eyelashes (long and thick, her only fine feature, according to her father) pulling her lids down like lead sinkers. They were leading her along the hard-packed dirt path to the front steps, one monk on each side, as if escorting her to a seat in the theater.

"What are you thinking of?" she had asked her father once as they sat together watching . . . what? A Shakespeare comedy, *Love's Labour's Lost,* that was it. Her father, as they changed scenes, sat staring as if hypnotized at the frail neck of the elderly lady in front of him, white hair wisping like smoke around her thin shoulders. "I could loop a rope over her head," he said. "She'd be gone before anyone knew. Never be missed." He smiled at her, but Emily turned away, not responding. She didn't like his mordant humor, was not convinced it *was* humor. Sometimes she thought, as she surveyed the daily disasters in the *Guardian,* that the wars covering the globe were simply extensions of her father's fantasies, his unhappiness. Why was it that when women were unhappy they thought of suicide and when men were unhappy they thought of murder?

"*Je ne suis pas fatiguée,*" Emily repeated drowsily. The monks had led her down a dank corridor with thin, cold radiators on the left and peeling rose-hued wallpaper on the right. Their sandals and her shoes made an enormous racket in the hallway. The room they brought her to was small, severe, but not unpleasant. They sat her down on a narrow bed with an iron bedstead, painted white, pushed against the white-curtained windows. A crude woodcarving of a weeping Christ hung over the bed.

" 'Ere you go, luv," the monk said, taking her by the heels and swinging her unresisting legs up on the bed. His powerful fingers seemed to be curled around her for a long time, and she fought to open her eyes and protest. She was afraid her dress was riding up again, but she was too exhausted to care and fell asleep with the two strange men bending above her. But even in her sleep she was afraid and could hear the rough voices of the men as they moved about the room, doors opening and closing. What were they going to do to her?

Much later, when she opened her eyes again, it was dark and she was sitting up in bed, clutching the bedcovers to her breast and looking out the window at a ghostly and unknown landscape. Her heart rattled; where was she? She remembered she had been driving to Mont St. Michel, and as she thought this she had the feeling that the covers were solidifying and she was holding on, not to blankets, but to the leather cover of her car's steering wheel. *Where was she?* At this moment the door on her right opened. Light poured in from behind, making the figure bending toward her a black silhouette, though he seemed to Emily to be vaguely familiar; and she reached out her hand for the last time.

The Starlings of Leicester Square

"I understand," the boy said. They were looking at a snapshot of four generations.

"No, you don't," the man said. "This was snapped right here in Leicester Square, in front of the statue of Shakespeare, because everyone thought I was a writer. I tried, but couldn't do it. I'd sit all morning and bang out a few lines, and everyone said they were terrific, but no one would publish them unless I paid for it. So everyone said you need an agent to get published, but you can't get an agent unless you're already published. I was a great disappointment to your mother. She thought she was marrying the new Shakespeare because I won the Senior Poetry Prize. It all seems bloody stupid now. For five years I sat at that typewriter with my thumb up my nose while your mother supported us. Have you lost your voice?"

"Hello."

"Jolly good." He had signaled the waiter in the Swiss restaurant to come over. "This wine is wretched," he said. "Bring us something decent: a Neuchâtel red, chilled." The waiter said nothing, but picked up the bottle and padded off. It was clear he didn't believe the man, who was dressed, below his good sportsjacket, in jeans and filthy sneakers.

"This is you," the man continued, "on my lap. You were a fat thing, and your head came out like a zucchini. And that's your grandpa, who is still a fat thing, and that proper English-man with the mustache and the stiff lower lip is your great-grandpa. Was. He never forgave me for marrying an American, and Jewish to boot. He told me it would never work out. Quite right, too. Would you like this picture?"

"I don't know," the boy said.

"Then to hell with it." The man crumpled the photograph and stuffed it in his cup of coffee, which spilled over the printed tablecloth. "If you don't want something hard enough"—his voice rose and diners at the nearby tables turned their heads—"then to hell with it."

The boy sipped his coffee and said nothing. He looked at the man steadily, without expression. He was a tall boy, pale, with brown curly hair and the faint beginnings of a mustache.

"That's what your mother did to me," the man said, "hardhearted bitch. Sorry," he added, as the boy raised his chin. "She did the same thing with old Rex when he got flatulent, just chucked him out. Said she couldn't breathe the air and he was staining her nice little ruggies. Waiter!"

The waiter stood silently, staring at the tablecloth.

"There's been a terrible accident, a frightful accident," the man said. "This time I'd like an Irish coffee, put in a double scotch instead of whiskey." The waiter carried away the cup with the crumpled photograph bobbing on the surface.

"But she liked this square, all the birds, all the trees— that's why I thought we could meet here. You've changed, you're looking more and more like her. Little eyes. But you're tall—in two years I'll be a shrimp next to you. She liked these big ugly knobby trees with the peeling bark and a thousand starlings on every limb, and I liked all the theaters around them, so it was a spot we could get together on. What do you feel, sitting here?"

"I don't know," the boy said again. "Nervous, I guess." He paused. "But not *very* nervous."

"Yes, just like your mother. She was not very anything. That's American, I think." He leaned back, waving his arms and teetering in his chair. "But we're all Americans now. We queue up for burgers and milkshakes and pizza and *Star Trek VII*. Bloody joggers all over the city, knocking down old ladies and picking them up again, nice as pie. Confess, you're a jogger, am I right?"

"Yes," said the boy. "I'm on the track team at college."

"I knew it. You have that lean and hungry look that worried Caesar. Do you think too much? Are you a dangerous young man?" He pulled out a mashed pack of cigarettes. "What kind of young man are you?"

"Just average," the boy said. "Not dangerous. I'm studying to be an engineer."

"Yes, all American boys become engineers, don't they? It must be a law of some sort. They build and they knock it down, they build and they knock it down. I would think it's exhausting."

"I have to go," the boy said, beginning to rise from the table.

"No!" The man put his hand on the boy's thin wrist. "Please don't go, it's been so many years. I know I'm not doing this well, I'm out of practice, is all. Don't go." The boy sat down again, but perched on the edge of his chair like a fledgling ready to test his wings. "Do you know what I do for a living?" the man asked. "Does your mother ever tell you how I make the money I send?"

"She says you do all right."

"I sell mail and laundry chutes to apartment buildings. It's quite profitable, actually. Better than bloody sonnets or short stories, what a fool I must have been! Everybody needs them—chutes I mean, not sonnets. Letters and dirty laundry, that's what the world's about. But at twenty-one"—he patted his pockets, looking for the photograph—"who knows that? And I think I was the youngest man ever to reach the age of twenty-one, I was that silly. Your mother liked that for a while, staying up all night to see the sunrise, sitting in the park waiting for the starlings to come out, things like that. You know what I like about you?"

"What?" said the boy.

"You look people in the eye, that might be American, too: the English have trouble doing that. We tend to stare at a light fixture while we talk, haven't you noticed?"

"You look at your drink," the boy said, and the man laughed, beckoning the waiter. "A pint of ale to stare at," he said to the waiter. He winked at the boy. "Never mix, never worry."

"That makes white wine, red wine, scotch, and beer," the boy said. "You won't get sick?"

"Sick?" said the man. "I'm dead. Your mother killed me. She was a keeper-tracker, too. 'That's your fourth,' she'd say. 'That's our sixth movie this month, that's the tenth time you said that, that's the twelfth time you've gone to the loo.' She got tired of my spending her money, I suppose; it must have bored her, cheering me up all the time. So she went back to Newport, la dee da, and took you with her. Do you like America, really?"

"I do," the boy said, "I like it a lot. I've met nice people."

"They're nice if you're not black or Mexican or Polish, whatever. Your mother told me some stories."

"Just read the papers," said the boy. "I mean the English papers."

"Yes, people prefer their own, don't they? Paint your bum green and sooner or later someone will shoot you. Only natural, after all."

"I really have to go. I have a date."

"Listen, did your mother ever tell you what we did the first time I was away from you? I flew to America; we had this crazy idea that American publishers would like my work better than the English publishers did. I was only going to be gone a week. You were about two years old and we were afraid you'd forget me, so we made a dozen copies of my passport photograph and pinned them all around your crib, probably scared you to death. Did she tell you that?"

"What did the publishers say?" the boy asked.

"Never saw them," the man said. "I stayed at the Algonquin and got terrified by the whole thing. I'd look up an editor's address and walk around the building and duck in the nearest pub for a drink. Came home in three days. She had taken down the photographs. You had eaten one of them apparently. She never told you that?"

The boy was standing, shrugging into his jacket. He took the man's hand. "Good-bye," he said. "Take care." He strode off on long thin legs.

The man turned around to watch him. He struggled to rise, then sat down again, pulling out his wallet. "He's a good lad," he told the waiter. "Did you hear him? 'Take care,' he said. He has every reason"—he held the waiter's eye—"*every reason* to dislike me. And still he said, 'Take care.' I bloody well will, too."

Through the windows he could see the starlings swooping and swerving over the bright marquees, in and out of the tall plane trees, mirroring the dense crowd below as we surged toward our dim and irresistible destinies.

Winter
Term

That January everyone in Paris was under thirty. The streets bustled all day, but about 10:00 P.M., when the first movies emptied, they began to hum with a special youthful energy. Knots of young people clustered around street musicians playing American rock songs, and others—like Sara, Giselle, and Nancy—sat in the windows of the cafés, nursing small coffees or inexpensive wines.

"I love Renoir," Sara said, her round face inscrutable behind large dark glasses. "He makes fat women so attractive." That afternoon they had been to a special Renoir exhibit with their art class and had agreed to meet in the evening for a blowout. It was Friday and they were tired of art. All morning they sketched, all afternoon they listened to lectures or attended exhibits. On weekends they took excursions: Chartres, Versailles, Rheims. And they had to do reading at night, all of it in French! This was an intensive one-month course, and though it was almost over—only the individual conferences with the instructor remained—Nancy felt she had bitten off more than she could *manger*. Her French was still minimal; she had trouble with languages, that was all there was to it.

Back in the U.S. she had even tried a hypnotist. "You are a little French girl," he told her, "learning to count: *un, deux, trois, quatre* . . ." It worked well for lists, even for verb declensions, but she was never able to put together whole sentences in actual conversations. She could only throw in nouns or verbs where they seemed most appropriate.

"*Les pommes,*" she said to her concierge this morning, pointing at a bowl of fruit in the concierge's kitchen. "*J'aime les pommes.*"

"*Vous parlez français très bien, Mademoiselle Nancy,*" said the old lady, who was overcharging her ten francs per night. But she didn't offer Nancy an apple.

Sara, on the other hand, spoke French fluently, almost as well as Giselle, who was married to a Frenchman and who had lived in Paris for six years. He called her Gigi.

"There are only three reasons why I stay in Paris," he told them one night in his soft accent. "*Gigi et Gigi et Gigi.* A young girl like her doesn't want to live in the country. But Paris is no longer the same." He often spoke of himself as an old man, because at thirty-five he was ten years older than Giselle. Nancy had disgraced herself that night by being unable to finish her dinner after Giselle announced, halfway through, that they were eating calves' brains.

"It's a *specialité* of the region where Henri is from," she said. "You were eating it before, what's the difference now that you know what it is?"

But Nancy thought she might get sick. "I know it doesn't make any sense; it's very good, really. I guess I've just had enough, is all."

They made an odd threesome, thought Nancy, who admired the others' sophistication, linguistic and otherwise. Sara was fat (as Sara herself said, there was no getting around it), and Giselle was headed in that direction, though she still could be described as lush. She was sexy, and dressed to show it. She had posed nude for Nancy and Sara; she enjoyed doing that, whereas Nancy would have fainted if they had made her do it. Maybe it was simply because, next to Sara and Giselle, she was built comparatively like a bird. In high school and college, shower time was never her favorite. Giselle's luxurious hair of groin and armpit somehow made Nancy nervous and self-conscious. Her sketches had been terrible.

Nancy had won an art contest in Providence, and the prize had been a round-trip ticket to Paris. A month was all she could afford, so when she found out about this Winter Term course she arranged with her university to get credit for it: it wasn't costing her much at all. In fact, compared to Giselle and Sara, she was the rich one, with her credit cards, checks from her parents, savings from her part-time job. Giselle was a full-time student and Henri an underpaid English teacher in a private Parisian high school; there was much talk of a book for children that Henri was working on and that Giselle would illustrate, but Nancy was skeptical. She hadn't seen any evidence of the book, and Giselle's style leaned toward the sloppy abstract and not toward children's illustrations. Sara's was a stranger case. She claimed to have met an Arab in Miami, where she was teaching in an ELS program.

"He's crazy about me," she told Nancy. "He said he likes legs that are so close together the wind can't whistle through! Isn't that crazy? I've been to Cairo and Beirut and London with him, and then he had to go back to his country. He would have sent me home, but I said, 'Just get me an apartment in Paris so I can work on my French.' " Nancy had doubts about this story, too—almost everything in Paris seemed unreal somehow—but Sara did have a nice apartment, although she never carried much more than twenty francs on her and apparently lived on *"croque monsieur"* sandwiches, the cheap toasted cheese ubiquitous in Paris, except when Nancy or Giselle bought her something more substantial. Nancy was happy to do this. She was flattered to be included in the trio, and they were making her experience Parisian.

Nancy stayed at a dumpy hotel near the Sorbonne, in the student quarter, where the view from her sixth-floor walk-up was magnificent; the rest of the conditions were, architecturally speaking, Late Bestial. By doing her studying in a nearby café and using the bathrooms in the museums, she was able to function fairly well. The best time was late at night when she could sit at her tiny desk and look out her window past the fussy but gorgeous facade of the Sorbonne to the illuminated dignity of the Pantheon. Since her *petit déjeuner* was delivered to her door at 6:30 A.M., everything about the month—the hours, the weather, the strain, the excitement—had conspired to make her pale and hollow-eyed, an effect she did not dislike.

"We'll never make it," Giselle was saying about herself and Henri. "I believe in evil and he believes in chocolate." The wine was making Nancy drowsy, but Sara and Giselle were becoming more animated.

"Evil and chocolate *belong* together," said Sara. "Remember *Candide:* it was necessary to get syphillis in order to get bonbons. Personally, I think it was worth it."

"You won't say that when your teeth drop out," said Giselle. "Right, Nancy?"

"You two are such charming conversationalists," Nancy said. "I think I'll throw up in my wine glass." Under the next table a large dog lay panting, his tongue unrolled like a carpet and hanging well below his chin.

"Well, it's almost eleven o'clock," Sara announced. "Time to meet my boyfriend. Want to come along? He said he might bring some friends."

"You mean the Arab?" asked Nancy. "He's come back?"

"God, no! If Yaseen knew I was seeing Tomas he would cut my belly open and offer you sausage."

"*Très jolie,*" said Giselle. "He sounds wonderful. Where are we going to meet these creatures of the night?"

"They should be at my apartment, if I can trust Tomas,

which I can't. But it's better than just sitting here on our last night together. He's fun, and his friends are, too. Tomas was born in Germany, but he's more French now. He's a translator and makes a lot of money."

Nancy already had drunk five or six glasses of wine; the evening was starting to move too fast for her to keep track. She felt heavy and dull-witted, and couldn't think of any sensible objections. She had gone to a few dances and met some boys at the art school; none had been interesting, but only one had been at all bothersome. Indeed he had chased her, late at night, along the Boul' Mich to her hotel, but he had been too drunk to be scary. Sara had asked, "Was he an Arab?"

"No, why should he be an Arab?"

"Nancy, don't be so innocent! An Arab can't go after his own women—her family would kill him—so he chases Europeans and Americans, especially naive Americans with pretty eyes." Nancy had very large blue eyes that Sara and Giselle were always praising.

She wasn't overly pleased to be going to Sara's apartment this late in the evening—how would she get back?—but the business of paying their bill and figuring out the tip kept her mind from focusing. Nancy wound up paying the entire amount, which seemed higher than it should have been; Giselle left a small tip, and Sara paid nothing. Well, why not? *Pourquoi pas?* She could afford it.

A cold drizzle blew over them as they walked to the metro. Nancy liked it; it sobered her up. Paris is *supposed* to drizzle, and Sara said tourists wouldn't complain about the weather unless children were drowning in the streets. A little damp doesn't matter, Nancy thought. On any corner look right, look left: the familiar and noble monuments confront you. No doubt about it, Paris was the most beautiful city in the world, and she was sorry her stay was drawing to a close.

Sara lived out towards the Bois de Boulogne, and by the time they got there the bells of the city were bonging midnight. The apartment was on the third floor of one of those old five-story buildings with art nouveau railings and windows. They could see from the street that her light was on. Nancy couldn't help feeling a surge of excitement: after all, she had come here (partly) to have adventures, rendezvous with romantic Frenchmen late at night. At the same time she could hear her father: When the head is a fool, the whole body's done for. But he had been talking about her decision to be an artist instead of a nurse or teacher. Nancy took a deep breath and, walking in the middle, linked her arms with her friends' and strode down the sidewalk, feeling on top of the world.

The apartment was dimly lit and a little cluttered, but neat and comfortable enough. Compared to Nancy's dingy hotel room, it was positively baronial: a heavy cocktail table covered with bottles and ashtrays, a deep sofa, four or five comfortable chairs. The bedroom door was open and the large unmade bed had a built-in bookcase as its headboard. The dining room and kitchen were small but had old cupboards and chairs: everything was in good taste. The walls were covered with matted posters of operas and art exhibits, including an eccentric and grotesque nude over the sofa announcing *Don Giovanni*.

The young men, Nancy thought, were a disaster. First of all, they were not that young. The only one her age, whose name was Adrian, was so drunk that he seemed retarded, though he was good-looking enough, small and slender with long brown hair. He struggled to stand up when they entered and an older man, laughing, pushed him back down on the sofa, where he remained sprawled with a full bottle of wine in his hand. She missed the older man's name, something like Auguste. He didn't speak English and she couldn't understand a word he said. He had a beefy build, graying hair, and an extremely florid face, as if his blood pressure was about to pop.

Tomas came over to greet them and kissed their hands,

lingering over Sara's. "We had despaired, my dears, absolutely despaired," he said. He kissed the inside of Sara's
elbow and smiled beatifically. He had the worst teeth,
crooked and brown, that Nancy had ever seen up close.
Tomas was a man of about thirty with a swarthy complexion
and receding none-too-clean black hair. He didn't look German to Nancy; more like a gypsy or—and this made no
sense, even to her—an underworld informant. He had a bobbing, ingratiating manner, smiled constantly, and was ex-
ceedingly amorous. Within fifteen minutes he had kissed
most of the available parts of Sara's ample body, and didn't at
all slow down his conversation.

"We are so happy you are to be here," he said, rubbing
Sara's hand against his prominent cheekbones. "We are the
luckiest gentlemen in the universe. And we have wonderful
things to drink!" He swept his hands toward the bottles on
the table. "Adrian has brought us a bottle of the very best
brandy, but we won't let him drink any of it; he's had enough
already." Adrian acknowledged this remark, tipping his bottle of wine toward Nancy. She could see that the party was a
set-up and that Adrian had been meant for her. That was all
right—she was rather touched by it, though she wished they
had asked her first. At any rate, Adrian was not about to
harm anyone; he was in worse shape than the fraternity
louts she was used to back home.

"Well, let's have some brandy then," said Sara, disengaging
herself from Tomas and going to the cupboard for glasses.
Tomas opened the bottle and poured five full glasses. Nancy
had never drunk brandy before, but she liked it. She could
feel it sliding down to her stomach, flooding her body, and
calming her nerves. Auguste had pulled his chair close to
Giselle, who was already laughing at his anecdotes. Nancy
couldn't just stare at the other couples, so she began wander-
ing around the rooms, sipping her brandy, studying the
posters.

After a while she heard Sara shout, "We almost forgot! It's time for our *formidable!*" At their favorite café the beer came in three sizes—*demi, serieux,* and *formidable*—and the three young women had pledged several times to drink a *formidable* together before Nancy had to return home. In the living room Tomas had lined up five huge steins and was pouring liter bottles of beer into them. Adrian apparently drank only out of wine bottles.

Nancy had misplaced her brandy, or perhaps had finished it, and now she was thirsty. But not that thirsty: she would need two hands just to pick it up! "No way, José," she said. "That thing is bigger than my stomach."

By now the smoke in the room was getting thick, as everyone but Nancy and Adrian smoked steadily while they drank. "Henri says that Parisians spit less than we used to," Giselle had said earlier, "but we still smoke like fiends."

Ne crachez pas, Nancy thought. Remembering this, she wondered what Henri was doing. Maybe he was out of town. Giselle and Auguste, if that was his name, were facing each other, clanking their steins together, his hand on her thigh, her hand on his stomach. Nancy gulped her beer. She was surprised to see it was well after 1:00 A.M. already, but she no longer felt tired. She wished Adrian were in better condition to talk; the others were so actively engaged. On impulse, she walked over and sat down near him on the sofa.

"That's more like it," said Sara, ducking away from Tomas, who seemed to be licking her face. "Here's to Paris. To Art. Cheers. Santé!" She tilted her beer and took a huge swallow. "Drink up, Nancy," she gasped, and Nancy drank as much as she could, some of the beer spilling over her chin and neck.

"Here's mud in your eyes," said Tomas, beaming.

Adrian straightened up, raised his bottle, and said, "Up your bottoms." He looked pleased as Sara and Giselle shrieked with laughter, raising their steins and repeating his toast. He looked at Nancy without smiling. "English good," he said. "*Un peu difficile.*" He slumped back again, keeping his eyes on Nancy.

Nancy, for her part, began to read the magazines stacked beneath the coffee table because it was embarrassing to watch the two couples. She felt like a Peeping Tom. Tomasina. The radio played loud music as she read an entire article, in French, about American jazz. Every once in a while Adrian would reach over for her hand, or arm—his aim was vague—and she brushed him away. She knew she was fairly drunk herself, but she felt reckless. After finishing the beer, she got up with a slight stagger and got a wine glass.

"Get me one, too, will you, honey?" said Sara. "One for Gigi, too." Nancy put the glasses carefully on the table and squinted at the labels. There were several different kinds of *Côte du Rhones* and *vins de table.* She picked up one with red wine and a label reading *de Granval.*

"Good," said Tomas, taking the bottle from her and pouring. "Seven francs a bottle, can you believe this? At these prices you're losing money when you're not drinking!" Everyone laughed except Adrian; Auguste laughed at everything, whether he understood it or not. His shirt was soaked with sweat. Adrian suddenly fell over, with his head on Nancy's lap. It startled her so much that she drained the whole glass of wine. Tomas grinned, refilling it. "Good, isn't it? Don't worry about Adrian. He just needs a good sleep."

"If he sleeps any better," Sara said, "he won't wake up."

Up close his face was quite nice, delicate, aristocratic in repose. His long dark lashes were dramatic against his white skin. His ears could be cleaner, Nancy noticed after a while, but outside of that . . .

Tomas picked up the magazine lying open beside her. "Listen to this," he said, reading, "women don't need the orgasms, after all!"

Was that what it said? Nancy had trouble lifting her head.

"Don't need it!" said Sara. "You mean I've been overachieving all this time?" A general babble arose, jokes, counterjokes, in French and English. Auguste sang a little song, not pretty, obviously ribald. Suddenly, Nancy realized, Giselle was taking off her clothes.

"Giselle will be posing for us!" said Tomas, applauding. "We shall take guesses. *Aphrodite! Olympia! Déjeuner sur l'herbe!*"

"*Odalisque!*" bellowed Auguste, across whose thick outstretched arms Giselle was hanging her clothes. All of this seemed perfectly logical to Nancy, who stood up, thinking she must go home, and instead wobbled past Sara and Tomas into the bedroom. He sat against the wall near the door with Sara sprawled between his outspread legs, his hairy arms around her breasts, his bad teeth showing as he watched Giselle.

Nancy stumbled head first onto the bed. As soon as she landed, the bed took off and began spinning over Paris, zooming with sickening speed by the gargoyles of Notre Dame and the iron edge of the Eiffel Tower. She dropped into the narrow lanes of the rue Mouffetard, face to face with gelatinous squid, fat fish with gaping mouths, rabbits swinging on hooks, and then lifted swiftly to a high plateau above the white dome of Sacre Coeur, the lights of Paris winking beneath her. Eventually she seemed to be flying out of Paris toward the huge cathedral at Rheims that somehow she could see in outline and in all its ornate detail at the same time. Far below, the cold squares of the winter vineyards, with their thin sticks lined up like crosses in formation, looked like gigantic graveyards in somber shades of brown.

For a while, then, she felt that she was in the great cathedral itself. It was cooler, and dark; she was being carried down the aisle to the altar and placed on the carpet there. The priest loomed, immensely tall, above her. He looked down at her, kindly, smiling. It was Tomas, and Nancy screamed.

"Hey, sweetheart, it's all right," he said. "Calm down."

Her dress was pulled up over her waist, and she was unable
to move her legs. A shirtless Adrian, expression vacant as
ever, was holding her ankles apart with terrific strength. Vio-
lent groans, apparently from Giselle, were coming from the
living room. Sara was sitting on the edge of the bed, a mound
of massive flesh clad only in panties. Tomas was the only
person fully dressed.

"Adrian's a good boy," said Sara, "be nice to him. He's very
rich." She rubbed her hand along Adrian's white back. "You
missed the big show. Gigi and Auguste posed for Rodin's
'The Kiss'—they were wonderful! You wouldn't believe
Auguste!"

"I have to go home," said Nancy, struggling to sit up. "Let
me go. I feel sick."

"No, stay with us, baby. You still have three days left in
Paris, you can spend them right here." Sara leaned down, her
moon face shining in the half-light; she began stroking Nancy's face, her other hand still on Adrian. Her large breasts
wobbled against Nancy's shoulder.

Nancy sunk her teeth deep into Sara's plump hand. She
didn't know how she did it, or exactly what happened next,
in what order. Adrian let her go at Sara's cry of pain, and
Nancy sat up. Certainly Sara slapped her, hard, across the
face, but whether that was before or after she got sick she
couldn't remember. She knew she knelt, retching, in front of
the toilet while Tomas stood holding her from behind, his
hands firmly upon her breasts. But he stepped back when
she got up.

She walked out. It seemed impossible. Do you just walk
out of scenes like this? Apparently so. She stood in the elevator for some time before pushing the button. When she
emerged from the building the gray light of early dawn made
the street ghostlike, pale and drowned. She forgot where the
metro was and began walking along the sidewalk, head
down, feeling that she should be crying, though she wasn't.

Eventually she came upon a café that was still open, or perhaps had just opened. It was almost deserted; two men looked at her without curiosity as she sat down and ordered coffee.

Nancy sat slumped at her table. Every part of her body ached, especially her eyes. She couldn't see right; she was probably still drunk and sick, and her head hurt where Sara had hit her. She felt that death surrounded her. The flesh on the man at the next table slid off his face like melting cheese. *Croque monsieur*, she thought, fighting hysterical laughter as the skeletons rattled their newspapers and coffee cups. She had made her first joke in French.

The
Water-Tree

He liked to sit under the water-tree in the cool of the evening, nursing a cold bottle of beer and smoking a cigarette. Mrs. Carlin didn't let him smoke indoors anymore. It was quiet here at that time, except for the soft sound of the water dripping from the blossoms, which smelled sweeter than the honeysuckle back in Georgia, although he supposed it wasn't really water dripping, but nectar. He liked the name: water-tree—there was something so elemental about it, like Africa itself.

Tonight the silence was shattered by the American group singing in Elizabeth Hall:

> I know a driver, mighty rash
> Hey la dee   la dee   la dee
> He almost broke my calabash
> Hey la dee la dee da

The raucous music made him feel old. He *was* getting old, he thought. At forty-seven he felt hemmed in, everything already behind him. He recognized this as unoriginal, irrational, and repetitious, but there it was. The skin in the crease of his elbow had that yellowish mummified look. Every night his wife came to bed with pink sponges in her hair.

That was why he and Mrs. Carlin had come on this trip, leaving the children behind with relatives. He was on a government study grant with other university professors, so he had only to pay his wife's expenses. It was to be a great adventure and perk up their lives. *Lions and tigers and bears oh my!* But it hadn't worked out that way. After three weeks in Nigeria, Mrs. Carlin wanted to go home. She was always sick, she hated the food—*monkey meat,* she knew it was monkey meat floating in that soup!—and the malaria pills disagreed with her. And so, while his wife went to bed early each night, worrying (with cause) about rats in the dormitory, Mr. Carlin sat under the water-tree in the university courtyard and drank a liter bottle of Star Beer and thought about Africa. He was trying to figure out why he loved it.

At first he thought it was because he had freedom here: no teaching, no domestic chores, no committee meetings or bridge parties. But he decided finally that he loved Africa because it was unstable: anything could happen. Society here seemed always on the verge of breakdown—coup and countercoup, gutted and abandoned houses with elegant carved porches, overturned Mercedes by the side of the road rusting in the April rains. And with all this, it had a positive energy that was missing in the States. For American society was also breaking down, and less excusably: corrupt politicians, greedy doctors, sleazy lawyers, lazy teachers, arrogant students, surly workmen. And unhappy children. His own son had been resisting his advice when they left.

"What do *you* know about life?" his son asked. "You've never done a damn thing!"

"I know you're like life itself," Mr. Carlin had replied. "Nasty, brutish, and short." His son had neither read Hobbes nor inherited Mr. Carlin's height.

In Nigeria, at least, the children and workmen *seemed* happy. But maybe he was wrong, he didn't know. Maybe he liked it just because Mrs. Carlin didn't . . . Mr. Carlin looked at his watch: 9:30. He had been thinking of going to the casino on the outskirts of town with Professor Giannino to watch the gambling. He had never been to a casino in his life, though in the army he had been a fair poker player. Gambling was legal in Nigeria and most of the large hotels had casinos as part of their attraction. Giannino, a young bachelor, had gone several times to the Hotel Internationale and had invited Mr. Carlin to accompany him the next time he went, probably tonight. But he was nowhere to be seen; perhaps he had forgotten his invitation and had gone off alone, as usual.

The casino opened at ten o'clock and Mr. Carlin didn't want to stay out past midnight: his wife would worry. If he was going, he'd have to go now. Impulsively, he finished his beer, left the courtyard, and walked down the broad flight of steps, immense in the fading light, leading to the guard-house where the taxis gathered. It was impossible not to think of the theme song from *Rocky* as he did so, and his step picked up as he neared the small queue of battered vehicles. He hadn't made up his mind to go, but when he reached the guardhouse he was surrounded by three taxi drivers clamoring for his fare, and the simplest way to stop them was to get into one of the waiting cars.

"How much to the Hotel Internationale?"

"Two naira."

"No, too much. Fifty kobos."

"I will take you for one naira, that's all."

Mr. Carlin knew he was being overcharged, by Nigerian standards, but $1.60 for a twenty-minute cab ride seemed reasonable to him so he settled back in his seat. When they reached the hotel the driver said once again, "Two naira."

"No, we agreed on one naira."

"Two naira, traffic bad." The driver began shouting, a mixture of Yoruba and broken English, gesticulating to the passersby and loungers in front of the hotel. "No pay, he no pay!"

Mr. Carlin hated scenes. He pulled two notes from his wallet, crumpled them up, threw them in the taxi window, and with flushed face marched across the sidewalk into the lobby of the Hotel Internationale. Heading straight to the bar, he ordered a double scotch, which they didn't have, and got a double whiskey instead. Stupid to get upset about a couple of dollars! But he was furious, thinking of various and better ways he could have handled the situation.

The bar was so dark that for a while he could see nothing. "And I Tiresias have foresuffered all . . ." he said to himself, quoting the only modern poem he was familiar with. Mr. Carlin taught European history, but having once had to wrestle with *The Waste Land* and *The Odyssey* in a Great Books course, tended to quote one or the other whenever he entered a darkened room. "So ends the bloody business of the day."

Ordering another whiskey, he got up and walked downstairs, following the signs to the casino. It was by now almost eleven, but when he opened the heavy leather doors he saw that the gaming tables were empty. Some people were drinking at the far end of the room, so—not knowing what else to do—he went over and sat down, embarrassed at bringing his own drink. There were six customers at the bar, two women and four men. Professor Giannino was not among them. Mr. Carlin sat between a black man in a tuxedo and the only white person there, who was speaking in German to the bartender. Mr. Carlin's German had never progressed much further than *"Wo ist der Bahnhof?"* but he listened attentively nevertheless. The German seemed to be telling a sad story, for the bartender's only contribution to the conversation was a series of sighs, rollings of eyes, and shakings of head. Perhaps he didn't understand German either.

The man on Mr. Carlin's right asked for a light and began to make polite conversation. He was a lean and handsome Nigerian, with two parallel scars etched into both of his cheekbones.

"I thought the casino opened at ten," said Mr. Carlin.

"O yes, the doors open, but no one plays until later."

The woman sitting next to the Nigerian leaned across him and said, "See, there are the dealers now." Across the room five men in dark suits were talking together at a table.

The Nigerian's name was Tom Adedeyo, and the woman with him was named Ayo; laughing, she wrote her name for him on a cocktail napkin. Regal and fierce-looking as an ebony carving, she had small well-formed breasts made prominent by her dress, which was dark blue, tight, and cut very low. When Adedeyo excused himself to greet some new-comers, Mr. Carlin found it difficult not to stare at her breasts as she leaned over to talk to him, and began gazing at her forehead with an effort of will that seemed ridiculous even as he was doing it.

By the time the lights brightened and the dealers had taken their places, the room had become more crowded, it was almost midnight, and Mr. Carlin had downed several more drinks. Though by no means a problem drinker, he loved his alcohol, not least because, compared to his friends, he held it well. But he was drinking faster than usual tonight, for two reasons. First, he was intimidated by the casino: he wasn't sure what the games were, how high the stakes; suppose he did something stupid, and lost all their money? There were five tables. One looked like regular three-card draw poker, one was blackjack, one he believed to be baccarat, and the other two he couldn't figure out. The tables were arranged in a circle, covered wagons huddling against an Indian attack. In the middle of the circle stood a high ladder-like perch, like a lifeguard's chair, on which two men sat back to back. *Riding shotgun*, Mr. Carlin thought.

The second reason was Ayo. Although attracted to many women, Mr. Carlin tended to be nervous when left alone with them. He had been this way all his life: he never knew what they were thinking. If his wife hadn't positively reached out and grabbed him, he would never have proposed.

He was almost handsome, a slim, tall, dark-eyed man who looked younger than his age despite flecks of gray in his black hair, and this partial shyness was part of his charm. Now it seemed to him—though he wasn't sure, what did he know about African women?—that Ayo was looking at him boldly, holding his eyes with hers whenever she could pry them off her forehead.

"What are you going to play?"

"I don't know, poker or blackjack," he told her. "I can't play very long. Where do you get the chips?"

"O I love to play blackjack! Come on, I'll show you." Ayo led him to a small alcove where an obese Nigerian sat with a stack of chips and a strongbox. You could buy two-, five-, and ten-naira chips, a minimum of twenty nairas to play.

Mr. Carlin took out his wallet. Twenty nairas was over thirty dollars! He had about a hundred nairas in his wallet, along with three fifty-dollar bills and a packet of American Express travelers' checks. But these had to last for more than a month, and he and his wife hadn't yet bought any of their gifts and souvenirs of carvings and fabrics—they were considering buying a statue of a snake magician, intricately carved from one piece of omoo wood, for which the artist was asking $150.

Well, what the hell, he thought—this was his one and only casino fling. He bought ten two-naira chips and gave five to Ayo. "Let's lose these and get it over with," he said.

"No, we're going to win!" she said. "You'll see."

While most of the tables were crowded, only one customer was playing blackjack. The casino used lean dealers and fat cards. The cards were the size of a paperback book. The dealer shuffled and handled them with speed and dexterity, pulling them from the bottom of a clear plastic container.

They each put out a chip. Mr. Carlin's down card was a six, then his up card a jack. "I'm good," he said. The dealer had fourteen, and pulled an eight.

"See, I knew we'd win," said Ayo.

Mr. Carlin kept winning. In a short time Ayo had lost all her chips. He offered her some more but she refused. "You're the lucky one tonight." Somebody kept bringing more drinks to the table.

He became absorbed in the game. He got two tens, split them, got another ten and an eight. He split the other ten and got a queen. The dealer had thirteen, pulled an ace and then a king. Mr. Carlin gathered up the chips. He began betting five-naira chips, won for a while, and then began to lose. He wanted to stop while he was still ahead.

"This is my last hand," he said, and he bet twenty nairas. The queen of spades, the ace of diamonds, his first blackjack, paying double, over sixty dollars. The dealer swiftly changed Mr. Carlin's large pile into thirteen ten-naira chips: he had won 130 nairas, more than two hundred dollars. Ayo linked arms with his as he cashed them in with the fat man in the alcove.

"We should have champagne! You were magnificent."

Although he found himself agreeing with her, Mr. Carlin looked at his watch and saw that it was 2:00 A.M. But he knew he had an excuse for his wife: he was winning, he couldn't quit, the casino stayed open until four o'clock. "All right," he said, "a bottle of champagne."

They sat at a small table in a dark corner of the casino. Mr. Carlin felt as if he were in a movie. He struck the matches for her cigarettes with one hand, a trick he had learned in the Army. The noise, the smoke, the lights in the room hummed and whirled. He felt light-headed but in control. They talked about Africa and he told her about the huge water-tree, how he loved to look at it, sit under it, listen to it and smell its fragrance. The more champagne he drank, the more he loved Africa.

Ayo was saying that she was hungry. He was, too. But no food was served in the casino at this late, or early, hour. "Come to my place," she said. "I can make us some sandwiches. I live very near to here."

The fog lifted from Mr. Carlin's mind for a moment. No, he had better not. And wasn't she with Adedeyo? O no, not at all, she had just met him here by accident.

"Well, I'll see you home," Mr. Carlin said. "But then I'll have to go." He didn't want to say it was late, he had to be in by a certain hour.

Outside the hotel he hailed a taxi, Ayo gave the address, and the old cab rattled through the twisting streets of the darkened city. He imagined he could smell the delicate scent of the water-tree even here, among the corrugated tin roofs and large stucco houses with broken windows and sagging porches. Here and there Mr. Carlin saw people sleeping on the sidewalk; occasionally a few furtive figures scurried along. In ten minutes the taxi stopped. "Wait here," Mr. Carlin told the cab driver as he got out with Ayo.

She lived in a square two-story house, a little run-down but with a solid tile roof and a number of large leafy trees clustered around it. These trees sheltered it from the neighbors and gave it a feeling of privacy, almost isolation. "I live on the second floor." Ayo took his hand and guided him to an outside flight of steps on the side of the house. The steps led to a small screened-in porch; he followed her through this into an interior room. The door was open and it was very dark.

In the darkness Ayo turned a half-step, into his arms. He swayed as he kissed her, almost falling down. The entire length of her body pressed against his, and when she at last stepped back he knew what was going to happen. He felt in a way that he deserved this, that perhaps everyone deserved this once in a while, a sort of noblesse oblige for the common man. He knew he wasn't thinking clearly, and when he felt her naked he stopped thinking entirely.

*   *   *

Mr. Carlin awoke to the cab's honking. He lurched up in bed, his heart pounding—it was almost 5:00 A.M., he must have fallen asleep an hour ago! Ayo wasn't in the bed; where was the other room? Mr. Carlin dressed hurriedly, fumbling without light, a sharp pain darting around his head. He looked for Ayo but was afraid to call out, and rushed from the room, through the porch, and stumbled down the steps to the waiting taxi.

"The University," he said to the driver, collapsing in the back seat. His head was going to blow off. They drove in silence for a while. Then the driver turned around and said, "This cost you very much. I wait long time."

"Yes, all right," said Mr. Carlin. "How much will it be?" He felt for his wallet and then yanked it out of his pocket. He couldn't believe it, he looked at it again and again. He turned absolutely sober. The wallet was empty. "Driver, turn around!" he almost screamed at the man. "Go back to the house we came from!" A little later he added, in a more normal voice, "I forgot something."

"This cost you very much," said the driver. Mr. Carlin held his head and began rocking back and forth, back and forth, like a man having a fit. When they reached the house he jumped out and ran up the steps and into the porch. The inside door was locked. He pounded on the door and after a while he heard slow footsteps approaching. The door opened part way. It was Adedeyo, still dressed in his tuxedo.

"Let me in," said Mr. Carlin. "I want to see Ayo."

"She's not here," said Adedeyo, not unkindly. "Go on home, it's late."

"Let me in or I'll kick the damn door down!" The force of Mr. Carlin's anger overcame all fear.

Adedeyo opened the door and Mr. Carlin rushed in, looked by the bed, in the bathroom, the kitchen. No money. No Ayo.

"I want my money, goddamn it!" He confronted Adedeyo.

"Get out of here," Adedeyo said. "You've had your little fun, as you Americans say, now get out before you get hurt."

He reached over and took Mr. Carlin's arm. With a cry of fury Mr. Carlin smashed his fist into Adedeyo's sharp cheekbone, sending him reeling backwards through the room. In a rage he charged after him, stopping just in front of the Nigerian as the faint light from outside glinted on the knife in Adedeyo's hands. And then Mr. Carlin dropped like a dead man as something crashed on his head from behind.

*   *   *

When he came to he was outside in a strange district. The sun was coming up a blazing red. Decrepit houses lay scattered around the landscape like abandoned machines on a battlefield. He was burning, he had descended into hell. *And the dead tree gives no shelter,* came to him, *the cricket no relief.* What time was it? His watch was gone, his wallet and his travelers' checks: all gone.

He had read somewhere that everything breaks down but the amino acids. Now he had a vision of the world disintegrating, everything crumbling into these irreducible molecules, whirling round and round the earth like the indestructible bones of witches. He lay down under a large tree. He knew he had a broken rib so he turned gingerly over on his back. The whole world continued to spin. After a while he could feel the sweet drops falling on his face.

The Bracelet

At first she had felt like a white fleck of foam in a black sea. She would bob along the crowded streets of the cloth market in Ibadan, looking at the bolts of bright fabrics piled higher than her head in front of the open shops lining the narrow dirt thoroughfares. She had been afraid to buy any of the beautiful material with the mysterious names—*adire, adinkra, kente, kyemfre*—because she didn't know how to haggle over prices and didn't want to pay too much. So she would just flow along with the crowd, small and wide-eyed, the lanes sometimes so jammed that her feet would be lifted from the ground and she'd be carried like a piece of driftwood with the tide.

But that had been ten years ago. She had come to Nigeria as an archaeologist working on her Ph.D. from the University of Minnesota. She had done some reading on the Old Kingdoms of the Yoruba and wanted to study them at firsthand, particularly the Kingdom of Oyo, one of the traditional centers of Nigerian culture. Ibadan was the natural place to go, an important market city with a new university, and it was less than twenty miles from Oyo, where they were reputed to still have slaves and eunuchs guarding the Oba's palace.

When she arrived Sally Warren was twenty-six years old. She was shy and quiet; at the same time, nothing much frightened her. She had a no-nonsense face with clear brown eyes that she didn't waste time gazing at. Her plan had been to spend a year or two researching the Kingdom of Oyo and then return to Minnesota and write her thesis. And then, she supposed, she'd get married. Her fiancé, Jim, was opposed to the trip entirely; he had wanted to get married right away. There was nothing wrong with Jim: he was fine, he was ambitious, he played a decent game of tennis. He was the type of young faculty member who was sure to advance, get tenure, and become chairman of his department. He had it all planned. Eventually they would have two baby archaeologists, a boy and a girl.

Sally was a reflective woman, but not a complaining one, even to herself, so the first time she realized that Jim bored her was when she was flying to Africa. They were flying over the vast expanse of the Sahara Desert; for an hour she looked at the unchanging, almost colorless sand. *Why, that's just like Jim,* she thought, and crossed him off.

Perhaps that was why Africa had given her such an enormous sense of freedom. She had no sooner taken a room at the University when her past years washed away like so many ridges of sand at high tide. Her room, on the second floor of the dormitory, was tiny: a bed, a desk, a wardrobe. An open passageway ran in front of it; she could bring a chair out there and look into the white flowers of a large frangipani tree growing in the courtyard next to the building. In the evening its jasmine-like fragrance flooded her room and she could think of nothing but the fragrance itself. That was what Africa was like to her: it demanded attention to the texture of her life.

For some time she pursued her studies at the University, with occasional field trips to Oyo, always made with great difficulty because of the irregularity of the bus system. To stay overnight in one of the cheap hotels was uncomfortable; she would be the only woman there, a white woman walking through a maze of small rooms where men sat silently drinking palm wine or chewing on kola nuts. At least they were always silent as she walked by, and even when she lay alone in her bed she felt them staring at her, their gazes a positive weight on her skin.

So her studies became diffused. As she got to know people at the University, some of whom had cars, she began visiting whatever places they were driving to. If they were going to Oyo, good; if they were going somewhere else, like Abeokuta or Oshogbo, good: off she went. She was learning a great deal about the Yoruba in general but not making much progress on the research for her thesis.

She made one marvelous find, by accident. She had been taken by one of the professors in the Institute of African Studies to visit an old shrine for Shango, the God of Thunder, which had been destroyed in a war but was still regarded as a holy place. It was outside of Meko and the jungle had almost reclaimed it. On the way back from the shrine she had gone off the overgrown trail to look at a small crimson flower she saw glowing in the shadows. As she knelt down by the flower her eye was caught by what seemed to be a tin can buried in the ground. When she pulled it up and brushed off the dirt and leaf mold, she found it was a brass bracelet about six inches wide, with intricately wrought figures and a series of small bells attached to either end.

Her companion was greatly excited. At first he thought it was ancient, but as they cleaned it he decided the bracelet must be between fifty and seventy-five years old, one of the ornate decorations worn by the priestesses of Shango or some related deity. He wanted Sally to bring it to the Institute for appraisal. "This is a fine discovery, Miss Warren, you're very lucky."

"I'll polish it up," she said, "and bring it over later."

But when she took it back to her room and worked on it for several hours, using a bottle cleaner, brass polish, and finally her toothbrush, she found she didn't want to give it up, or even let it out of her hands. The bracelet was a perfect fit, feeling heavy and snug on her arm. There was a long mirror on the inside of her wardrobe door; she stood in front of it with the bracelet on, and then slowly took off her clothes and looked at herself for a long time. *Maybe I'm going off my rocker,* she thought, and smiled. But she began doing this every night, sleeping naked under the mosquito netting, wearing only the bracelet.

The months slid by. She made two good friends, both of them dancers, with whom she would take her meals in the University dining hall. Andrew Cage was a thirty-year-old Englishman who had studied medicine at Oxford and switched to dance late in his student career. He had danced with several of the major companies in England and America and had come to Ibadan two years before to study African dance. Like Sally, he found much that fascinated him, but his specific studies went slowly. Unlike Sally, however, whose money was running out, Andrew seemed to have a decent independent income, and he often paid for all three of them when they went out together.

The other dancer was Manu Uchendu. Manu was the son of a chief of one of the larger villages in northern Nigeria. Despite his small stature, he was a commanding presence: slow and oracular in talk, dignified and erect in carriage, he looked the part of a chief. His eyes were deep-set and yet prominent; he was almost pop-eyed. *High blood pressure,* said Andrew. But he inspired confidence; when Manu spoke in his measured, musical tones, people edged forward to listen.

When Andrew spoke, people tended to laugh. He was cynical and worldly, and often drunk. Sally thought he might be homosexual. Once she asked him why he had never married. "It's the old story," he told her. "*I* loved her. *She* loved her." And that was all she could get out of him on the subject. But he was careful not to be alone with her at night.

One evening Sally brought him to her room to see the

The Piano Tuner

bracelet; he was edgy and uncomfortable. "Yes," he said, when she put it on. "You're a natural priestess. I wish you'd put a curse on old Millers." Millers was the stuffy director of Andrew's dance project. "May his tongue swell and his genitals wither." Andrew wouldn't sit down in those close quarters. He went out on the passageway and stared at the frangipani tree trembling in the moonlight.

One Sunday Manu told them that the fetish priest of a small village near Oshogbo was going to perform, that this was "the real thing" and they should try to see it. "We'll have to bring him some sort of gift, like a bottle of schnapps, that's customary."

"I've got a bottle of Gilbey's gin," said Andrew. "I can teach him how to make a martini."

"Gin will be all right; just let me handle it."

They drove in Andrew's car. The village consisted of several clusters of mudbrick huts with rusted corrugated tin roofs sprawled around an open market. One cluster enclosed a small courtyard where a crowd of villagers, mostly women, were already assembled. Manu spoke to one of the elders, who placed the gin by a large handcarved chair with wooden snakes forming the legs and arms. The three visitors sat down at the edge of the circle of people.

Four drummers had been playing softly in the background; now their beat became faster and more insistent. The crowd stirred as the priest entered the compound. He was a little old man completely covered with a gray clay-like substance, snakes wrapped around his neck, wrists, ankles. There was something wrong with his face—eyes and mouth twitching—and his limbs trembled in the heat as if he were freezing. "Parkinson's disease," murmured Andrew. The priest sat in the chair, one gray leg shaking violently, and received gifts from the village women: yams, cloth, pineapples, a large white chicken. He brandished a pair of brushes made of cowtails; beside him a young man held a basin of white

148

powder. As each woman presented her gift, she would touch the ground in front of the priest and he would chant to her, dipping the cowtails in the powder and brushing her shoulders.

"He is curing sickness," Manu whispered. "And barrenness, and back luck. He can only do it when he's possessed."

"I don't feel well myself," said Andrew. "I could use some of that gin."

Sally was spellbound. She was trying to commit every detail to memory. She wondered if she would be frightened if this were at night.

The drums became more and more excited. With dignity the priest stood up and began to dance, stamping and shuffling in a circular motion. He took a banana and rubbed it over his face and body, then did the same thing with several eggs. Now his young helper handed him the fluttering chicken. The drummers leaped up and began playing in a frenzy; the priest whirled around, swinging the chicken over his head. He stretched the chicken to its full length and sank his teeth into its neck, tearing at it until he put the chicken's head into his mouth and bit it off. Blood streamed down his neck and torso. Still dancing wildly he again swung the chicken around, ripping off its wings and legs, blood spattering the spectators.

As the tempo of the drummers slowed, he turned and stopped in front of Sally. Without hestitation she stood up, then touched the ground with both hands as she had seen the women do. He brushed her shoulders with the white powder, chanted for a minute, and it was over.

Back in the car they were silent for a long time. After a while Sally asked, "What did he say to me?"

"He wished you good health and asked the gods to watch over you here in Nigeria," said Manu.

"It turned my stomach," said Andrew. "I've read about geeks in American carnivals, old winos who bite the heads off chickens for a few drinks. I don't know how you stood up when he came to you."

But Sally was elated. She felt that she had done the right thing, that something significant had happened.

Not long after, Manu became Sally's lover. He seemed to expect it, he didn't press her. They were in her room, talking about her plans, about the experience with the fetish priest; she was wearing the bracelet. When he held out his hands, she went to him, her body pushing at him of its own volition while her mind thought *Why not?*

It didn't seem to make any difference in her life. They were careful; she wasn't swept away by passion. Sally had learned long ago to dismiss all generalizations: they were fine, you needed them to hold a decent conversation, but they never applied to a particular case, to her case (even this generalization, she realized, was suspect: perhaps some *did* apply to her case). Jim had been a great generalizer; he had theories about everything. But she had never understood theories. As soon as she uttered or wrote one, the exceptions would crowd into her mind like a mob of unruly children clamoring for attention. This trait wasn't helping her write her thesis.

So one day at a time the year disappeared. The University of Minnesota renewed her scholarship for a year, but even so she was hard-pressed for money. Jim's letters, frequent at first, slowed down to a trickle, though he threatened to fly to Ibadan to find out what was wrong with her. But Sally was sure he would never do such an extravagant thing, even for love. After about a year and a half at the University she began looking for a job. She worked for a while as a cataloger in the University museum: this wasn't bad work, but consumed a lot of time. Work on her thesis had virtually stopped.

Then one afternoon Andrew had come running in with a great announcement. "I've found just the place for you," he yelled from below her balcony, "and it's free, too!"

He had discovered a large abandoned house outside of Oshogbo, near the Oshun River. Years ago many people in the house had died of the plague, and the natives believed it to be inhabited by evil spirits. But the chief of that district paid a man and his wife to guard the house, and they lived in a little hut on the same property. Andrew was sure that if Manu would speak to the chief Sally could live in the house for nothing, they could fix it up for her. It was the perfect place for an archaeologist as there were many shrines, both active and abandoned, in the area around the river.

Gradually it was all arranged. Near the end of the second year of her stay Sally moved into the Oshogbo house. It was a three-story affair with an ornately carved roof and a porch on the second floor as well as the first. A dirt road around three miles long joined it to the main highway leading into Oshogbo, and it was less than an hour's drive from Ibadan and Oyo. The three friends painted it and fixed the windows, and chased away the family of monkeys living on the third floor. They stocked it with food from the University commissary, and Andrew brought over what looked like a five-year supply of bandages and other medical provisions, and a ten-year supply of candles.

For a short while Andrew and Manu stayed with Sally, Andrew sleeping in a room on the first floor and Manu and Sally sharing the master bedroom on the second. They swam (and washed) in the slow-flowing river, explored the territory and the neighboring shrines, and in the evening danced by candlelight in the large and empty main room on the ground floor. It was a good time, but when the men left to return to their studies Sally looked around at her house and felt exultant. She thought that she always knew that people were essentially alone, and she liked it that way. She remembered being puzzled by movies and books in which men were punished by being placed in solitary confinement. "That wouldn't bother me at all," she said to a large green and orange lizard. "I would prefer it." And she raised her arms and whirled around the room, the bracelet picking up the candlelight and refracting it on the ceiling and walls as she danced.

A few days after Manu and Andrew left, Sally heard activity in the courtyard. A man and a woman were erecting a series of bamboo poles near the native hut. These must be the caretakers who were not in evidence when she moved in: Sally hurried down to greet them. The woman turned slowly around and bowed her head. She was a large woman, a head taller than Sally, and her hands and feet were stained a dark blue. Her name was Vida; she and her husband Ayi had gone into Oshogbo when Andrew's car appeared and had just today decided it was safe to return. By now Sally could speak some Yoruba, and Vida knew a little English from three years in a government school, so they were able to communicate without difficulty. Ayi was a farmer who worked a small plot of land about two miles from the house. He planted mostly yams, but also grew corn and beans and sometimes melons. Ayi even owned several kola trees and sold kola nuts as his main cash crop.

Vida brought in some money by making the traditional Yoruba cloth called *adire*, which accounted for her blue hands and feet. One reason she and Ayi stayed on a place thought by most to be haunted was the great profusion of the *elu* plant on the property. Vida would take the fresh green leaves and pound them into a blackish pulp, making a high pile of dye balls about the size of tennis balls. Sally was fascinated by the whole process of dyeing and soon was helping Vida regularly with her work. Andrew or Manu would arrive for a visit and find her tying or folding the lengths of white cotton that Vida would then dip in the large dye pots half buried in the ground. Around the courtyard lengths of the beautiful indigo blue fabric with their intricate designs were drying on the bamboo poles.

"I love doing this," she told Andrew. "I could do this forever. I can already tie the *osubamba* design." She pointed to some drying panels with large white circles surrounded by many small ones. "Big moons and little moons."

"Pretty nice," said Andrew, "but I'm not sure how I'll like you with blue hands and feet." The *adire* dye was very hard to get off; the ground by Vida's hut was stained a permanent blue.

Sally tried to get Ayi and Vida to move into the house with her, but they would have none of it. They thought Sally blessed by the gods to be able to live in the house unscathed. In fact, it was clear they saw their roles as handservants to her. Ayi brought her food from the farm, Vida cooked it; once every four days they would clean the first floor of the house, though it scarcely needed it. They wouldn't go upstairs, and they wouldn't enter the house if Sally weren't in it. They had set ideas as to what kind of work was appropriate for her. It was fine for Sally to work hard tying and folding the *adire* designs and helping with the dyeing process in general, but they didn't like her to carry things, to cook, to sweep, to pound the yams and cassava for the *foofoo* which was their staple meal. In a very short time a peaceable and efficient routine was established.

Sally liked walking to the cloth market outside of Oshogbo, where Vida would sell their work and buy the raffia string and the white cotton they used. One afternoon on the way back from the market she met a woman with a sick child. "She's burning up with fever," Sally said, her hand on the child's dry forehead. She brought them home with her and treated the child as best she could—she had learned a lot from Andrew—giving clear directions to the mother for continued treatment. A few weeks later the woman returned and left two large water pots on the porch. As the year progressed there were more of these incidents. Sometimes women from the small neighboring villages would bring their children to the house. They were afraid of the large hospital in Oshogbo, though they would go there if Sally told them to, and they would never stay in her house.

"They think you're a priestess of Oshun," Manu told her, looking at the pots, carvings, little brass figures, and river-worn stones that were collecting on her porch. "Oshun is the Venus of Yoruba, almost as light-skinned as you; if she feels like it she can cause or cure dysentery, stomachache, stuff like that. She was one of the wives of Shango, you know, very famous for her lovemaking."

Sally smiled. "Well, let's see if I qualify," and they went upstairs.

Manu had studied the art of divination and he taught the rudiments of it to Sally, using sixteen kola nuts which could be thrown or arranged in any number of combinations. In college Sally had learned to do the *I Ching*, and this was similar; she memorized the verses and chants for the different combinations with great ease. "You're a born diviner, a *babalawo*," he told her. "It's in your bones."

Sally believed in it, in her own way. She thought it as good a way of regulating one's life as any other. She remembered reading about one of those English archaeologists with the hyphenated names like Pritchard-Evans or Evans-Pritchard, who lived with a tribe somewhere that made its decisions by poisoning chickens with a poison called *benje* and then de-ciphering the circular patterns in which the chickens ran as they died. The Englishman had lived this way himself for a year and claimed it was about as efficient as trying to reason things out (Shall I go to market today? Shall I plant my vege-tables? Should I marry Alice when I return?).

*   *   *

In this way, time had gone placidly by, like the Oshun River flowing by her house. Tonight, holding Jim's letter in her hand and looking back on her ten years in Africa, Sally had difficulty remembering what happened when. Andrew was dead, she knew that; he had gone back to England and then died. And she hadn't seen Manu for a long time: he had returned to his village in the north to become chief. He told Sally that she could be one of his wives any time she wanted. She thanked him and thought she'd rather not. "You could be one of my husbands, though."

"Yes, I'd like that."

But it had been several years since she had a visit from Manu. Now her house was truly like a shrine, surrounded on all sides with the artifacts of Yoruba life and religion. The monkeys had moved back in to the third floor and were her pets. At night they would look out the windows when the young men stood before the house, silent in the moonlight; occasionally the door would open and one would enter . . .

The University had long since severed its connection with Sally, so she had been totally surprised a month before when its mail truck came bouncing down their road with a thick letter from Jim and one from her father. Her mother had died, they wanted her to come home; her mother had left her $10,000. It seemed strange to her that she had parents; they had never captured her imagination, one way or the other. Jim hadn't married; he had been engaged (*engaged?* Sally could barely understand the word) several times, but it had never worked out. He was a disappointed man. He wanted to see Sally again. When she opened the mail her hand trembled; she didn't know how she felt. After reading the letters she took out her sixteen cowry shells and began to arrange them, searching for an attitude. She loved the small brightly colored shells that someone had left for her to do her divinations with. She would hold them in her hands for hours, their smooth, highly polished surfaces somehow comforting her, joining her with the hypnotic rhythms of the sea. But the shells had said nothing but "Wait," and so she hadn't answered the letters.

And now Jim's second letter had arrived today. He and her

father were at the University and would be coming to get her tomorrow. They were terribly worried, they had heard awful stories, they feared for her life. Sally smiled as she read this.

The moon was caught in the branches of the God-tree, the three-forked tree leaning over the river which flowed silently and irresistibly toward the great ocean. She walked upstairs to her room and stood for some time looking at her face in the mirror. She piled her long hair on top of her head. She was wearing one of her *osubamba* cloths around her waist; multicolored beads which the women had left for her hung between her naked breasts, and the bracelet felt cool and solid on her arm. Then she took out the narrow file she had borrowed from Vida and began filing her front teeth into the traditional M-shaped gap of Yoruba women.

Previous winners of
THE FLANNERY O'CONNOR AWARD
FOR SHORT FICTION

David Walton, *Evening Out*
Leigh Allison Wilson, *From the Bottom Up*
Sandra Thompson, *Close-Ups*
Susan Neville, *The Invention of Flight*
François Camoin, *Why Men Are Afraid of Women*
Mary Hood, *How Far She Went*
Molly Giles, *Rough Translations*
Daniel Curley, *Living with Snakes*

PS3563 E348 P5 1986
+The piano tuner +Meinke, Peter.

0 00 02 0300919 6
MIDDLEBURY COLLEGE